2016

Writing from Inlandia

An Inlandia Institute Publication

Editorial Board

ISBN: 978-0-9970932-3-0

Inlandia's Workshops: A History

During the summer of 2008, a group of writers came together in Riverside. Led by Ruth Nolan, the resultant workshop became the first Inlandia Creative Writing Workshop. That summer, participants' writings were gathered into a chapbook, "Slouching Toward Mt. Rubidoux Manor," which launched with a reading to a packed house at Back to the Grind in Riverside in 2009.

Participants came from all over the region to attend this workshop. One of those participants was Jean Waggoner of Idyllwild. Recognizing a need in her community, she formed a second Inlandia workshop, which she later co-led with Myra Dutton. The next year, Cati Porter formed a workshop in Ontario. Around that same time, Maureen Alsop formed one in Palm Springs. Learning there was a need for a workshop in the Corona area, Matt Nadelson stepped up. Then came Andrea Fingerson and our San Bernardino workshop emerged.

In the span of eight years, we had gone from one workshop to six. The program was thriving. The anthology, by necessity, grew. Marion Mitchell-Wilson, Inlandia's founder, dubbed this newly expanded anthology Writing from Inlandia.

Lives change. People move on. When Marion became ill, Cati moved into an administrative role, and Charlotte Davidson took over Ontario. Maureen moved on and so Alaina Bixon took over. When Alaina left, Jean Waggoner picked up the slack by combining Idyllwild and the desert to form Shadow Mountain. When Matt Nadelson took a teaching job in San Pedro, Andrea Fingerson took on Corona in addition to her San Bernardino group.

Again this past year, we have seen additional changes: Jean retired, so we lost Shadow Mountain, but welcomed Nikia Chaney to lead San Bernardino. We also adopted an existing group in Redlands, led by a longstanding workshops participant Mae Wagner. This year also saw Charlotte Davidson's retirement, but with it, the addition of Tim Hatch.

The needs of a community change as it grows so we added focused Boot Camp for Writers workshops, led by Stephanie Barbe Hammer (poetry), Yi Shun Lai (epistolary), Tatyana Branham (short fiction), and Minda Reves (memoir). We also continued our partnership with the University of California, Riverside's Gluck Fellows of the Arts program with poets Nicole Olwean and Emily Dorff for a National Poetry Month workshop series, plus Nikia Chaney led a wonderful Poetry off the Page workshop series.

The purpose of this anthology is to celebrate the writing and writers of our region. The work that you read here is just a slice of all the good stuff that this region has to offer.

Read local. Support local writers. We are making history.

Appreciation

This anthology would not exist without the talented and dedicated writers and workshop leaders who participate in Inlandia's Creative Writing Workshops Program, a sampling of whom appear here. It is only because of their hard work, and the time and dedication of Inlandia staff, committee members, and volunteers, that this anthology was compiled, formatted, proofread, proofread again, submitted for review by the writers themselves, corrected, reviewed again, and then finally submitted for publication. Without that time and dedication we would have nothing to show for a year of good, productive writing—except, of course, the writing, which, thanks to all of them, you can now read here.

Inlandia's programs, including the annual publication of the Writing from Inlandia anthology, are made possible by grants from the E. Rhodes and Leona B. Carpenter Foundation, the City of Riverside, and Poets & Writers Readings/Workshops Program, with particular thanks to the director of their west coast office, Jamie FitzGerald Lahey, and the James Irvine Foundation, funder of Poets & Writers Readings/Workshops Program. We also wish to thank Inlandia's members for their generous donations of time, talent, and treasure. Special thanks to our readers for appreciating the good work found here.

We also wish to thank our host venues for allowing us to use their space to hold our workshops: the Riverside Public Library downtown, the Corona Public Library, the Rowe Branch Library in San Bernardino, the Palm Desert Library, Joslyn Senior Center, Riverside Art Museum, and the Ovitt Family Community Library in Ontario.

We are grateful for all of your support.

—Cati Porter, Executive Director

Contents

2016

Writing from Inlandia

Celena Diana Bumpus

Three Reflections

(Three Interconnected Tanka)

VESSEL

Stained like a cloudy
sky-- sitting high on the shelf.
Your grey ashes filled
the round, smooth crevices and
the void in our memories.

SHATTERPROOF

Resilient heart.
I bounce when I'm tossed away.
Boomerang upon
return. Aim at any chest,
hoping to cohere.

CRUTCH

I lean heavily
on you, afar or near. Your
cardamon voice soothes
and smoothes creases from my tight
brow. Hermetically sealed.

Celena Diana Bumpus

Picante

(In honor of the San Bernardino California Conservation
Corps chefs)

Bursting with tomatillo
Recipe borrowed from
Mexican immigrants
The secret?
Fire roasted chiles and
Yellow Bells
Each bite makes you
Thirst for water and
Cling to sweetness

Celena Diana Bumpus

Five Interweaving Rabbit Tails

(Five Haiku)

White rabbit sits in
void between traffic sounds. She
counts cars and not sheep.

Metronome headlights
both blind and comfort. Wheels on
pavements share sagas.

Neon lights intrigue
the small rabbit, whispering—
"Adventure within".

Car horns give warnings
the white rabbit disobeys.
Life gives challenges.

Daylight breaks. The sun,
a hazy question mark, floats.
Rabbit ventures forth.

Celena Diana Bumpus

Poolside

Mahogany eyes set just a little farther apart
than most, inside a caramel macchiato face
with the barest hint of whipped cream.
Her pomegranate lips stretched tight over
her pearly white smile. She strains to cover
her childlike giggle. She looks at me lounging
fitfully next to the glimmering hot pool.
My skin burnt to carob by the harsh Riverside
sun. My eyes hidden behind my oversized
sunglasses, dreaming I was at Balboa Beach
watching the waves crash like cymbals
on the giant rocks.

Celena Diana Bumpus

Breaking Rules

(For W.)

Loving you is like free falling from a HALO drop only to
release a parachute with tangled lines. You are the adrenaline
rush I have craved. Though I see nothing below in the the
darkness dribbling from the open door of the C-130. I know
somewhere beneath me is terra firma. Questions hover...

Do I crash land?
Will I be rescued by my backup parachute?
The wind shear blinds me. Somewhere on Earth
I know you wait for me. Loving you is a constant battle
of trust. You love me like I'm your last breath,
but you would die before you uttered those words.

Celena Diana Bumpus

When Our Lips Meet

Shh mmm shh
Sloop nngh grr sloop
Falloop mm fallope ahh
Purrr assem purr assem
Huck grrr sloop nngh
Falloop mmm fallope ahh

Celena Diana Bumpus

Blow

(For Q.)

I was a new balloon in a package
sitting on the shelf for too long.
He was the hand that pulled apart
the plastic, the air that blew
into my body, stretching, filling.

Celena Diana Bumpus

Solace?

(For W.)

And who's to say what a heart deserves or doesn't deserve?
Who's to measure true love born of conversations in cars.
It's that moment when we both are too raw, still struggling
with the words that we fall helplessly into each other's arms.
Gratitude is mistaken for love. Compassion is confused for love.

And yet, with all this time apart, my obsession with you has
waned. Your face fades from memory as I wander through the
house. Cobwebs clinging in the corners of rooms I seldom
visit anymore.

4:30 A.M.

(For W.)

Awake for 36 straight hours, I am circling inside this tornado of fear, desire, passion, frustration, confusion, and hope. I'm intoxicated by this perceived perfection between us.

The strange dichotomy between you and I is that in person we translate nearly as seamlessly as we do on the phone. My lips drawn to your lips and my tongue straining to duel with yours. You are this masterpiece of intellect, imagination, wit, humor, beauty and grace I do not want to stop myself from exploring.

I want to dive into you like you are the Caribbean Sea: impossibly clear with schools of fast moving cobalt and daffodil colored fish, it's cadre of sharp biting jellyfish, it's Grand Canyon aquatic depths, and waves that roll across your body like smoke from a fire.

I am both so out of control and so in control I don't know how to do anything other than read your mind and anticipate your needs.

Every time your rum-flavored gaze captures mine, I see a reflection of all of those wishes in a mate mirrored back at me.

"Am I afraid of being happy?"

If I carry any fear it would be in wanting to shotgun my heart into believing it is already in love with you. It's this double edged sword I find I want to cut myself with every time I steal a moment of space to think about you. I want you to want me more than anyone you can ever imagine wanting in your life.

I want you to crave contact with me as though it was each breath you savor. I want you to look at me and think "Mine". I want to beg you help me to understand that I am not sailing in this ship alone.

And maybe it's a matter of trust. I would trust you with my heart. But, know that it is both fragile and strong. I struggle not to mold myself into you but to fold my heart into us.

Please have mercy on my lack of eloquence. My heart and mind are too focused upon you to remain speechless.

You See

(For W.)

Our love is this falling crow,

      this talking bird, sliding down

      the currents of the wind.

      This black feathered being

      that has forgotten

      how to save itself.

Our love is this koala bear

      drunk on Eucalyptus

      with claws the envy of any feline.

      Its loaded, Cheshire Cat smile

      Beckoning you close

      to rip you to shreds.

My love is the elephant in the room.

      The elephant who forgot

      how to be an elephant,

Cumbersome, alone and graceless

searching for her herd--

someone, anyone, to give her

a semblance of place.

Your love is this rust colored fox.

Crafty, shy and hiding

always peeking at me

from a distance.

Following me in silent steps,

imprinting my scent

into memory

in our fleeting moments together.

My heart is this snowy rabbit

Hiding in plain sight

daring to be noticed,

yet inconspicuous.

The very action of

my stillness

makes me blend more

into your background.

Deenaz P. Coachbuilder

Between God and Me

Regard with tranquility
the life that swirls around you.
Understand and acknowledge
your imperfect nature
your innermost nature.
You are, as all mortals, vulnerable, incomplete
a pear bruised at the edges.

How do you measure your life?

I see many lives in my life.
Capricious gentle child,
elastic adolescent
insatiable, inquiring, learning, adapting,
questioning you,
my faith and the trappings of gentility.

An industrious, successful professional
who made her way
with restraint and some dignity.

A woman fortunate to be loved
and who loves wholly.

Continuously striving to address the hurt in existence.

The faults that trap me are mine
for surely, in a hundred ways
I should try harder.

Cancer permanently altered me.
You let me live,
now, my being
a general condition of love,
for there is no ordinary.
I feel this throbbing incandescent universe
in my marrow
"fresho kereti", a blissful state,
achieving in uncertainty
a stillness of being.

My pen records the residue of angst in my heart
exposing and making articulate my inner life.
It explores the world's wrongdoing and rightdoig.

My paint brush dips with delight into the gentle currents of life.
I see movement and vast unreconciled spaces.
Myriads of interlocking colors shade
the chambers of my heart.

God, will that not be enough?

The answer must come
in your very heart
in your very heartbeat.

The poem was written in response to a prompt, "Write a poem to God or a God figure" in a creative writing workshop led by Jo Scott-Co in the fall session of 2015.

Deenaz P. Coachbuilder

Soul Song

dedicated to all grandmothers

The magical music inside me
swirled around Barjor's*
warm body
on my lap
resting lightly
against my chest
seated on the piano stool
my finger over his
tapping out happy birthday
his tight dark curls
tickling my chin.

The piano played happy birthday, he said.

No, I say silently
that is my soul singing.

*Barjor, my grandson was three years old

Skin deep

"You are becoming as brown as a berry", my mother would say with concern, for we all knew that many Indian men preferred light skinned women. I would traverse the tree lined avenues of Mumabi, India, with my friends, stopping at sidewalk cafes and eating street food cooked off the pavement, then fresh coconut water with its skimmed creamy insides, and often a stop at our favorite shop for sweet cold paan*.

My college friends were Hindus and Muslims, Parsis, Sikhs, Christians and Jews, from North Indian Kashmir and Delhi, to South Indian Tamil Nadu and the coasts of Kerala and Andhra. They were burnt umber beautiful from the south, and green-grey eyed Kashmiri sirens from the plains and plateaus of the Himalayas. Differences of religion, community and skin color unnoticed, we mingled, dreamed and schemed together, believing that we would conquer the unfolding years.

My son, relatively fair of complexion, met, wooed and married a beautiful African American. After hours of a difficult labor during which I heard the heartbeat of this reluctant being-to-be magnified in the delivery room monitor, who worried about what our grandson would look like? We just wanted a healthy baby.

And there he was, a perfectly formed angel, soft wavy hair, skin as pink as pale rose petals, the edges of his ears and feet multicolored with little dark patches. An artistic sculpture rather than a living thing.

Over the months his coloring changed, like the unfolding stages of a painting, not pink anymore but a delightful creamy complexion, matching the darker coloring of his infant ears and feet. Those wavy locks though still soft to the touch like the kiss of fine mist, have turned into lush tight ringlets.

I, who had never noticed skin color, am captivated with this changeling.

Only his eyes remain the same. Dark brown, intelligent, wary, sensitive.

*Paan- a preparation combining betel leaf with areca nut, a mouth freshener

Deenaz P. Coachbuilder

a dew

r

o

p

dawn's dew
forms along
greened branches
trickles down
collects
in tree forks
transforms into
a translucent
shimmering bubble
increases
heavier
elongates
droops
dips lower
until
it
b u r s t s
s h a t t e r i n g
into a myriad
rainbow crystals
captured
in Aurora's
resplendent ray

Deenaz P. Coachbuilder

and they live

as long as the living
go on living
the dead
will be alive
reflected in
the constellations
the continents
in a home
a room
bed
in quiet dreams
folded within
the heart

Deenaz P. Coachbuilder

The runt tree

I saved you again today from being dug up and discarded,
Magnolia with stunted limbs and scraggly leaves struggling to unfold,
so dear to me. You were one of nine healthy and flourishing trees,
planted in an imposing row against the gleaming backyard fence.

All your relatives are resplendent of foliage, the burnt umber underside
of their leaves contrasting sharply against their shiny sap green fronts
pagoda like seed pods bursting with potential life
swaying and chanting a hushed song in the summer breeze.

Your leaves chatter and shiver. Your slim trunk shudders
as if a gale were buffeting your very existence.
Shorter than your companions, you paint an uneven skyline,
marring the carefully planned symmetry of the garden.
Not a tonic of Vitamin B, nor an extra dose of cool, life giving water
makes a difference, your shy diffident spirit hidden and
almost forgotten, eclipsed between the vigor of the others.

I am aware of you, inexplicably, your difference a magnet.
I sense how valiantly you try, your continued existence an anomaly.

I too had young students who attended a school I worked in,
neglected at home, living in the midst of unpredictability. No kiss
ushered them to school in the morning, hidden in a pocket
a *Fravashi,** a good spirit to guide them through the day.
One young student's brother was shot and killed as they
rode their bicycles, close to home. One's father was in prison,
another's just…missing. One young man was being reared
by a great grand mother. They adored each other. She would attend

all parent trainings, falling gently to sleep slumped against my shoulder as the discussion unfolded.

Some came to visit us after graduating, sensing that behind our smiles was a silent prayer,
>   as is mine for you, Magnolia.

*Zoroastrians believe that every being has a Fravashi, a guardian angel that guides one along the right path

Forgive

You who died on my doorstep,
fine tapered bill
bluegreen iridescent hummingbird

whom neither the quickening sun
nor my frantic tears could awaken,

leaving your little nestling waiting anxiously
in the tiny beige home so painstakingly constructed
in the courtyard hibiscus hideout

did you not think
that I would awaken

night after night
haunted by your absence

ah, with sugar water, I tried

forgive me,

forgive.

Deenaz P. Coachbuilder

Forever Cherished

Familiar books rub shoulder to shoulder
along the crowded shelves of my family's library.
Six thousand volumes collected across decades.
New leather bound sets gleam
their vivid colors a magnet to the eye.
Some are covered with shards of dry broken
paper fragments, frayed edges filled
with tiny worm holes.

Many are childhood gifts from parents and friends
for books were preferred birthday presents,
looked upon with anticipation as that favorite day approached.

Each conceal a story,
a long forgotten gift inscribed with love,
tokens of lost friendships,
first editions hunted down in unfamiliar bookstores,
their ribs and inside covers kept carefully clean,
forever cherished.

Oh the hours of pleasure they exuded,
instigators of unparalleled imagination
ignited through time and space.

Our Mumbai house is to be sold, the precious library's fate
in my reluctant restless hands.

Treasured memories whirl around my senses,
their tendrils clinging.

As I glance through lace curtains
gulmohor blossoms dot the sky like a murmuration
of migrating starlings.

The evening flees.

Deenaz P. Coachbuilder

Thanksgiving

Thank you for the gift* of the world,
the mourning dove's
plaintive salutation of dawn
that seeps through my window,
the world's symphony transformed
into arias of winged souls,
splash of tumbling water,
a goods train's rumbling clatter.
For many years
I did not hear its song.

I had a cherished dog whose golden eyes
spoke to me of ancient stories.
He meets me in my dreams.

Flinging my arms around
an ancient California redwood
I learned to hear its heartbeat.

I have lost and loved and lied and learned,
have harvested and burned.
You gave me a lasting love
a lover with whom to grow.

Mine is a mind that finds no rest
a spirit that strives towards
space and quietude.
Mine the mistakes
that return and those that escape,

thank heavens, no ownership of just desserts!

Thank you for a grandson's
damask cheek, curly hair
his trusting fingers clinging to my hand
the pure luck that is the gift
of his toothy smile.

Thank you for the myriad words captured
in Scheherazade's tales,
poems that haunt
that echo in the heart.
They spread like an invisible carpet
across the miracle that is my life.

Thank you for the friends who stitch
each fold of fading yesterdays
into tomorrow's crystalline sunrise.

*To a cancer survivor each new day is a gift.

California Christmas

SOUTHERN CAL CHRISTMAS
Folks coming in from the fringe of the desert
Down from the North Coast, up from the border
Happy to be in the home we all love
With people who "get" our sense of humor.

TRAVELERS' CHRISTMAS
Gifts from Athens and Istambul
Exotic spices and harem pants
Scarves and pashmina from Kashmir
Olive oil and soaps from the Turkish baths.

PATIO CHRISTMAS
Tables laden with appetizers
Tables burdened with holiday feast
Tables loaded with desserts and champagne
We can sit down but we can't get back up!

CALIFORNIA CUISINE CHRISTMAS
Strawberries in the cranberry sauce
Chorizo in the stuffing
Chipotles in the chile relleno casserole
Grilled and smoky veggies—yum!

CALIFORNIA DIVORCE CHRISTMAS
Everyone's there but my husband
I'm in Carlsbad with my kids and grandkids (and my Ex)
He's in L.A. with his kids and grandkids (and his Ex)
Eating tofu and kelp.

CARLSBAD CHRISTMAS
Eighty degrees in the shade
Shorts and tees, tennies and hats
Wading low surf to the Oceanside pier.
Anyone dreaming of a white Christmas?

Laurel V. Cortés

Slumgullion
or
Don't Bring Any Friends Home
To Dinner Tonight

During World War II, when the U.S. government rationed so many foods, my mother would sometimes call us in to eat with one word: "Slumgullion!" Now as then, slumgullion is the crazy dish you make the day *after* you think you are "out of everything." It consists of bits and pieces of food found in your refrigerator and pantry, probably cooked in and served from your large frying pan. My Mom never wasted a thing, and I didn't fall very far from her tree.

The word "slum" was a nineteenth century British slang word meaning "back room" until Charles Dickens ascribed to it a darker, more colorful meaning, as "down a scary back alley." It has devolved from that into meaning a tortured, devastated area of town. I hate to tell you that the word "gullion" started out meaning "cesspool." The two words joined together hardly form a promising description for the evening meal!

Slumgullion is always a surprise. You never quite anticipate what leftovers lurk in your kitchen. There is that bit of pepperoni, an apple, the last chunk of the delicious flap meat you ate on Tuesday, one green onion, one-half of a red pepper, a few dried cranberries, a tablespoon of sour cream, some leftover rice, 2 oz. of cheddar cheese, and a bag of potato chips they gave you at Panera: that's it! So sauté the fresh foods, add the cooked foods, sauces and spices, sprinkle the grated cheese and the crushed crunchies on top, and you have… slumgullion!

Hobo stew and Brunswick stew share a history with slumgullion. In many places during the Depression the homeless were allowed to build fires. In a large cast iron pot suspended over the fire by pipes or branches found by the wayside, they made a communal stew. People contributed what they could beg, borrow or steal: two carrots from one man, an onion from another, a stolen chicken if they lucked out, otherwise just vegetables and scraps of meat--perhaps something handed to one of them on the street by a compassionate housewife. Everyone shared in the feast. There might be fruit and hoecakes for dessert, especially after the harvest, when gleaning was permitted.

More recently, when we still had a cash-only economy, here is what would happen: there was great meat on your menu during the first week and a half, casseroles (with actual recipes) for two weeks and eventually--just before payday--slumgullion. Nowadays, if you are one of those who pay for groceries by credit card throughout the month, slumgullion time comes whenever you are just too lazy to go to the grocery store.

The truth is, I don't mind saying to my husband, as my Mom said before me: "Dinner will be ready in a minute. We're just having slumgullion." He knows what kinds of things we have been eating, so he invariably says, "Sounds good. Bring it on!"

Laurel V. Cortés

The First Thanksgiving: What Really Happened

Imagine feeling relieved that your small company of 50 souls, including only five of you women, had finally settled into a tiny, newly-built village comprised of seven English-style thatched-roof houses, a common hall and three storehouses. Your experience living on a ship in the harbor for the entire past winter was devastating; fully one-half of the 100 men, women and children on board had died from exposure and disease. No family was spared a heartbreaking loss.

Imagine that a bilingual native to the area named Squanto—recently returned from his second abduction to Europe--had given you the courage to go on; he taught your community farming, fishing, cooking and coping techniques for this complicated new land.

Then what if one day in early fall the governor of the colony, John Carver, and the head honcho of your neophyte village, Captain Myles Standish, decided that there should be a harvest feast, ordering you five women to create a menu using the completely unfamiliar bounty the men had just dropped off at your doorstep. Ah!! And they've invited a few guests!

Now consider the possibility that this group of strangers turned out to be 90 more men—natives to the region--who were used to attending harvest feasts lasting three or four days. Can't disappoint the guests! For the men: food and drink, fun and games lasting three days; for the women and few older children: scary servitude. Not only that, but you five lonely and still grieving women worried about using up provisions harvested and stored for the much-dreaded fall and winter ahead. It had already turned ominously cool in early

October.

"140 mouths to feed!"

"Who's used to doing this kind of work?"

"Who knows how to cook these strange things?"

(Certainly not you or anyone you knew in England.)

"Who's going to take care of the babies?"

"We're already overworked on a normal day, including feeding 50 people 3 times a day."

"We just got off the boat and I don't like this place!"

"It's a good thing that we are Puritans, or you might hear what we really think about this deal!"

"Is this a nightmare?"

No, it was all too real. The village was Plymouth, Massachusetts, the year was 1621, and the event is now known as The First Thanksgiving.

Were these five women busy during those three days? Well, with the wringing of necks, the plucking and prepping and spit-roasting of many exotic wild birds, including big-breasted turkeys and quail they stuffed with nuts; ducks and geese; manipulating one of the five deer the Indians donated; cleaning the many creatures pulled from the sea, including crabs, oysters, bass, codfish, eels, scallops, clams and late-season lobsters-- yes, they were busy. They roasted ears of corn, and iron kettles suspended over the fires held stews of many kinds and the succotash, clam chowder and corn-based Indian pudding they were still learning to cook under Squanto's direction. They baked corn biscuits and cornbread over the hearths in the houses and hoecakes in the ashes to accompany the many meals.

During the course of the celebration, the women put nuts and drying ripe fruit--cherries, plums, gooseberries and strawberries--into corn dough for desserts. Craneberries (their bushes reminded one of cranes) were too bitter to eat without sugar, and there was no sugar. Red and white "sweet and strong" wine that the women made from the abundance of local grapes, along with "strong waters" brought on the Mayflower from beyond The Great Pond, helped the men to wash it all down.

They set the meals out on planks placed over sawhorses. While the women and older girls rushed around, the eleven dozen feasters sat on logs or tree trunks (with the Indians on the ground as was their custom). Using the few available knives to carve the meat (since there would be no forks in America for another dozen years) the celebrants mostly ate with their hands or with spoons made of clam shells--scooping the stews out of trenchers carved from tree trunks.

The men and boys' games included bow and arrow contests among the Indians, leaping!, jumping!, racing! and playing stool ball, which was akin to croquet. Captain Standish's stalwart militia entertained the company by parading, bugling, and firing off volleys of blank ammunition. Oh, these men were exhausted (not to mention drunk)! Time for a nap! --while the five beleaguered women and their youngsters cleaned up and wrung and plucked and prepped for the next meal.

"Let's do this *every* year!"

Sadly, there was no harvest feast in 1622. As the women feared, the Pilgrims indeed suffered deprivation during the second long harsh winter, so the colonists ate the summer food as it ripened. The storehouses were again depleted.

But the vision of Myles Standish and his light-hearted crew and the ninety Indian braves enjoying the Big First Feast in enlightened harmony has lingered on to this day in our fond collective memory. But who bore the brunt?

Soon the recently widowed, middle-aged, short in stature (the Indians called him "little man"), scruffy, rough-speaking Captain Standish asked his young scholarly roommate John Alden to choose the right words to promote Standish as a husband to Priscilla Mullins. Miss Mullins, at eighteen the eldest and prettiest teenager in the village, was orphaned when her parents died during the brutal winter on the ship.

The task was agonizing for John, as he himself was smitten with his young friend, the only eligible girl in the colony. But he chose to honor loyalty and friendship above his own wishes and spoke on behalf of the leader Standish, praising his heroic accomplishments on the battlefield. The level-headed Priscilla's immortal reply, "Why don't you speak for yourself, John?" sealed the deal, and she became Mrs. Alden in the early spring of 1622.

Should we be shocked by her choice? Captain Standish was not a dear friend of Miss Mullins. No doubt she primarily viewed him as a military leader who had thoughtlessly imposed that 80-hour ordeal upon the few surviving women and young girls of the village of Plymouth! Would you be tempted to marry such a man?

Thanksgiving week hasn't changed much for women since 1621, except perhaps for that exceptional number of guests and a lack of bugle music in the background (the football game on TV must now suffice). But honestly, the first Thanksgiving was harder on the five immigrant women than we ever imagined, and don't you sometimes just wish that all the history books weren't written by men?

Cape Horn

Cape Horn protruded, suddenly and dramatically, from the low-hanging morning clouds. There it loomed, to the right of our cruise ship -- tall, stark, craggy, mysterious, ominous, taunting, mesmerizing. The Horn lurched unpredictably as the jagged dawn waves relentlessly battered our ship, tipping us from side to side, front to back, into new angles, with moments of foreboding calm shattered by blasts of Antarctic winds.

"Everybody, please stay inside," came the captain's Norwegian-tinged caution on the loudspeaker.

Too late. By then Laurel and I, along with some three dozen others, had taken up residence on the ship's highest outer deck. We had come too far not to immerse ourselves in the pulsating crossing of Drake's Passage, the world's most turbulent conduit where the Pacific and Atlantic Oceans wage eternal, nearly ceaseless warfare, trapped in an unforgiving arena between Antarctica and the southern tip of South America. This experience, both exhilarating and terrifying, has been celebrated in such accounts as Sir Francis Drake's chronicles and Richard Henry Dana's *Two Years Before the Mast.*

We laughed uproariously as we sipped our once-hot drinks, tightened our grips on the railing to keep from falling, and huddled in our layers of sweatshirts in an effort to protect ourselves from the icy winds that whipped through us at their whim, shifting force and direction without remorse. Then the ship began to turn slowly to the right. No longer following a course parallel to The Horn, the ship headed straight toward our journey's target, intent on giving us a close-up of its majesty.

The altered course had thrust the Crow's Nest lounge directly between us and The Horn, so Laurel and I headed inside to enjoy its inviting environs -- a large semi-circular room with curved, wrap-around floor-to-ceiling windows. Here we could restock our drinks, partake of the breakfast buffet, and get a better view of the rapidly advancing cliffs. Relaxing in the Crow's Nest we watched in awe as The Horn approached, arrogant and undefeated, observing our ship's struggle with muted insolence.

Suddenly The Horn disappeared, as the ship's prow jerked, then rose majestically, spilling coffee, eggs, and sausages into our laps. Then back down . . . and down and down, until we were staring directly into the abyss. Cups, plates, and donuts flew toward the front windows, now covered with a spray projected from the sea. Up again rose the prow, then down again, each change of angle creating additional turmoil in the Crow's Nest and, as we later learned, throughout the ship, including knocking out power to the elevators.

"Oh, oh," came the Norwegian voice. "We're getting out of here." The ship turned again, now distancing itself from The Horn, which soon began to recede.

As the Crow's Nest made the transition from spasms into a more rhythmic, more predictable rocking and rolling, we all howled with laughter. We had survived The Horn. This called for refills, although we had to tread carefully to avoid the chaos on the floor.

Again the Captain's voice rejoined us. "Is everybody O.K.?"

We looked around. My eyes -- not alone -- turned to the empty deck where a few minutes earlier we had been cavorting, then down at the sea, then back to the bar to determine if all of our friends were there. As we perused the environs to see if anyone was missing, the Crow's Nest turned silent. I took Laurel's hand.

Carlos Cortés

When You Come to the End of a Perfect Day
(with thanks to Carrie Jacobs-Bond)

When you come to the end of a perfect day
And you don't want it ever to end
Then you try to find ways to lengthen the hours
And look for the moments to bend.

It is then that you peer at the resolute clock
And you know that your efforts will fail
So you smile at the lady who sits by your side
And accept that your boat will soon sail.

When you come to the end of an imperfect life
You forget all the things that went wrong
And instead you take joy in your memory world
As you leave with a touch and a song.

Carlos Cortés

Retirement Haiku

Being retired
Means each time I'm re-tired
I can take a nap.

Ellen Estilai

Resignation

I will not be your Comma Queen.
Let Vision Guy, if he's so keen,
defer grand dreams and strategies,
pick up his Bic and intervene.

I will not wrangle passive voice,
or in subjunctive mood rejoice.
Let Action Man engage, bestir,
restrain, subdue his verb of choice.

I will not will myself to fight,
to edit text into the night.
Big Picture Boy can stet and fret,
illuminate and make it right.

I will not say they are inept
whose grammar books were lightly kept.
But I maintain they overstepped.
Is there a motion to accept?

Saffron Prayers

My new favorite Persian word is *ghalambor*. It used to be *zaferaan*, or saffron, but after reading my friend Bahram's article on the ney, the reed plant, I am partial to *ghalambor*. It is a graft of two words, *ghalam*, a reed pen, and *bor*, from the verb *boridan*, to cut. A ghalambor is someone who, with a sharp knife and steady hand, fashions reeds into the pens used by a calligrapher.

I like the fluidity of *ghalambor*, the way it catches at the back of the soft palate in an uvular plosive--almost a gagging sound to the Western ear—then skims the alveolar ridge, and pauses between compressed lips before gliding out on that final, accented syllable—open, soft, unfettered by the final "r." *Ghalambor.*

It's my new favorite word as much for its sound as for the surprising obviousness of it. The word is not even in my *Haïm's New Persian-English Dictionary*, but it should be. As much as I've admired the acrobatic, layered lines of Persian calligraphy, I never thought about the centuries of pen cutters who made them possible. Apparently, Mr. Haïm didn't either.

This oversight made me feel guilty and sad for the forgotten and marginalized *ghalambor*. It made me think of Rumi's poem about the Persian reed flute, cut from the same reedbed as the *ghalam*. Rumi says the flute's mournful sound is the cry of the reed longing to be reunited with its reedbed. Does the *ghalambor* long to be reunited with his pens? Does he long to write his own story?

This is the kind of melancholy that calls for saffron. *Zaferaan* and saffron, its softer English equivalent, are still favorite words—conjuring up languid Friday lunches with fragrant, steaming, saffron-laced rice. After years of cooking with saffron, I thought I knew all about it--how to grind it into a fine powder before dissolving it in hot water; how much to use before it becomes bitter and overwhelming; how, with the right person and the right paella, it's an aphrodisiac. I knew that the ancient Welsh used it to cure melancholy, and that Iranians believe too much of it could cause a person to die laughing. But from one of Bahram's books, I learned something else: to dispel unhappiness or grief, some devout Iranians write prayers in saffron ink, soak the prayer sheets in water, then drink the saffron-tinged liquid left behind.

The *ghalambor* should do this. The pen cutter should become the penman. He should grind the saffron the way a calligrapher would grind pigment for his ink. Inhaling the honey-sweet saltiness, he should steep the powder until the water turns sunset orange, then wet the sharpened reed he kept for himself and write prayers of remembrance. He should bear witness as the marks he made swirl away into amber water, then drink the diffused prayers--prayers for the lost reeds and prayers for himself, that he be remembered.

Ellen Estilai

Tenants Leave

Whatever
you want to do with this stuff
is your business—
closet doors derailed,
armless ceiling fans churning impotently,
loamy mound of garden soil in the driveway—it's
organic, by the way.
And the clothes we put on to play house,
shed along with our student selves and
shoved in a pile in the living room (that doubled as a
bedroom for all the people who weren't on the lease),
You can have those too.
Or give them to the needy.
Whatever.
We won't apologize for
rusty crud under the toilet rim or
crusty film on the windows or
musty margarine in the fridge or
dusty drawers full of tedium.
This is life.
We've left you the brown couch with mystery stains,
and the IKEA outlines in the carpet,
like a crime scene.
(An apt allusion, don't you think?)
You can have the cleaning deposit and the
chart of chores—an ironic artifact you probably won't
appreciate.
This is business.
Business has risks.

We learned that in Econ.
Lessee, lessor—loser.
Whatever.
We couldn't remove
the stench of snark,
the funk of frivolity,
the patina of privilege.
We can always make more.

Ellen Estilai

Walk-Ons

Scene One, Ellwood City, PA, 1951:

The small girl with chocolate curls, her mother, and her kitten watch the neighbor's grandson play with his dog in the yard across the wire fence. The kitten crawls through a hole in the fence and makes its way through the tall, sweet summer grass to the boy and his dog. The boy picks up the kitten. The dog advances, barking, jumping. The boy drops the kitten in front of the dog. The girl and her mother watch as the dog tears the kitten apart.

"Look at its eyes!" cries the girl's mother.

Later, the boy will deny dropping the kitten. Years later the small girl will remember the first time she saw someone lie and get away with it.

Scene Two, Seattle, 1953:

The hall monitor is doing her job. She stands at the top of the stairs during recess and says to any child at the bottom of the stairs, "Whatareyoucomingupfor." The young girl with brown braids and a crooked part waits, scuffed shoe poised on the first step, her skinned knee bleeding. "Whatareyoucomingupfor," says the hall monitor.

The young girl, blood collecting in her white sock, climbs the stairs and walks past the hall monitor without answering. Years later, the girl will remember the day she understood that bureaucracy is unimaginative, and she will know that this is what she was coming up for.

Scene Three, San Francisco, 1967:

The man in the Greyhound bus station cafeteria sidles up to the young woman with long brown hair sitting alone, careless of her powers, eating a slice of apple pie. His stringy hair is slicked back, and he has fresh scratches on his face.

"I would like some pie," he says.

"I would like to be alone," she says.

Years later, she will wonder if the person who scratched him was even more careless than she.

Scene Four, San Francisco, 1967, later that same day:

The young woman with long brown hair, still careless of her powers, glides past the window of Caffe Trieste in North Beach. A thin man with a silk paisley cravat and a large boil on his nose dashes out of the café and asks her if she would like to come in for a coffee. Years later, the girl, now a woman with shorter brown hair and diminished powers, still wonders how men who wear cravats and carry warning signs on their faces can be so optimistic.

Scene Five, Los Angeles, 1971:

The young wife and her husband sit in the crowded LAX departure lounge watching a middle-aged man and woman with New York accents wage a loud argument. They play to the crowd. With every barb, like bad vaudeville actors, they sneak a peek at their audience and smile. Years later, the young wife, now middle-aged with hair that is no longer worth mentioning, will find herself in another airport lounge with that same husband, unsmiling, engaged in an argument for which she is relieved there is not much of an audience.

Scene Six, Ontario, CA, 1974:

In a different airport lounge, a tall, elegant young woman with long blonde hair, crisp blue blazer with gold buttons, and immaculate white pants, looks up from her magazine and says to the stranger sitting next to her: "Please put out that cigarette." He wastes no time grinding out the stub in the nearest ashtray while she turns back to her magazine. The youngish woman watching this encounter, having bypassed power suits on her journey from bohemian to matronly, knows that she would sooner move to another seat than make such a request. Years later, she will find her version of the voice that makes people do what they would rather not do, but she will never master the power suit.

Scene Seven, Toronto, 1990:

The old woman in a gray coat wheels around a Toronto street corner so fast she nearly runs into the young American woman and her family looking in the shop windows. "Move!" she growls. From this one syllable, the American woman knows that the old woman is Italian, her kitchen smells of anise, sausage and fried peppers, and her family is afraid of her. Years later, the American woman's kitchen often smells of anise, sausage, and fried peppers, but her family is not afraid of her.

Scene Eight, Paris, 1997:

The handsome flight attendant praises the American woman for studying French on the flight from LAX to Paris. While she reviews the subjunctive mood, he makes sure her wine glass is filled, jokes with her husband, makes them feel special. They connect. As the American woman and her husband leave the airport, they see the flight attendant enter a glass elevator. They smile at him as he ascends. He sees them but looks away. His shift is over. *C'ést la vie.* Years later, the woman realizes that when you let a language slip away, the subjunctive is the first thing to go.

Nan Friedley

Puddles

"The world is mud-licious and puddle-wonderful."

—e.e. cummings

Raindrop collectors
filling empty spaces
that meld together
growing deep and wide.

In my high heels
I walk around them
step over them
careful to miss them.

I reflect in the mini pools
a younger version of me
proudly strutting
my soggy socks.

Remembering a time
when I wore the badge of mud
on my white rubber boots
champion of jumping in
with both feet.

Fearlessly running through them
creating a wake in my path
bravely splashing waves
that touched my smile.

Nan Friedley

Big E Test Fail

squinting on the front row
tilting my head, hoping
the blurry letters on the board
would magically become unfuzzy
Miss Cummings knew

my deception was publicly
exposed in second grade
by our school nurse
when I could only read

T O Z

line three on the eye chart

no one else got one
the "you failed" letter
the "call the doctor quick
your kid can't see" letter

I wanted the blue ones
my mom picked white ones
cat-eye frames with rhinestones
I hated them

bifocals, old-lady glasses
worn in merciless middle school
girl bullies in their prime
self-esteem plummeted

finally, contact lens
financed by my first job
store cashier at sixteen

I couldn't stop smiling

Nan Friedley

Band Director

an extra-curricular job
assigned to not-yet tenured teachers
decided in a September staff meeting
by snickering peers.

Our instruments were black song flutes
and the bandroom was a renovated
storage closet next to the office
empty with the exception of fifteen
metal folding chairs and a music stand.

My deaf students played eagerly
covering tone holes
with their awkward fingers
feeling the vibrations of the shrill sounds
they created in the windowless block-wall room.

They blew into their flutes
with abandonment, not grasping
the importance of *pianissimo.*

I earned my small stipend
allocated for band director
almost equal to the amount
I spent on aspirin.

Nan Friedley

Picture Day

Fidgeting in alphabetical
order, craning their necks
to see past the spotlights
and movie screens, makeshift
studio in the school library

clutching their Lifetouch™
order forms
boxes checked for mom's
choice of pose
classic mottled blue background

I. Garcia is first to smile
wearing a white button-up
with a splash of hot sauce
from this morning's
breakfast burrito

V. Lozano, 42 BMI score
in her spaghetti-strap top
purple tutu skirt
over flesh-toned leggings
teetering on two-inch heels

say *cheese*, J. Spencer
missing two front teeth
liberally applied gel
creating slicked back
immoveable hair

S. Walker needed do-overs
looking out the window
rocking on the step-stool
blinking at the camera

And me
just remembered I wore
this same shirt for last year's
picture day

please don't share
your black plastic combs

Nan Friedley

Short Yellow Bus

Her mom packed her breakfast
Fruit Loops in a ziplock bag
to keep her busy
on the ride to school.
The driver said "no food"
but would always give in.

Systematically she ate them.
First pink, then purple, blue, green, orange
in sequential order until her least favorite
yellow was left.
Those she dumped on the bus floor.

She carried an adult-sized
hand-me-down backpack
for her collections:
scraps of paper
pens and pencils
books
unusual rocks she coveted.

Rocking quietly in her front row seat
colostomy bag connected
blind in right eye
prosthetic left leg
replacing her amputated one
AFO's for both feet
she smiled…a private joke.

On her more agreeable days
she'd sing the "Alphabet" song
in her timid voice
pointing to imaginary letters
or count to 100
on the bus window's condensation.

Most days she tried to trip
fellow passengers
boarding the bus.
If successful she squinted her eye at them
flashing a satisfied smirk.

She used her removable leg
as a weapon on substitute teachers
a "missile" on less than compassionate bus drivers
her tiny demonstration of control
in a world where she had none.

Nan Friedley

Lounge Lizards

"If I were not president, if I were King in America, I would abolish all teachers' lounges where they sit together and worry about 'woe is me'"

-John Kasich

water cooler
for teachers

central hub of mailboxes
phone messages from parents
Xerox™ machine churning our copies
paper cutters, die-cutters
tools of the trade

adult-sized toilets
for bladders trained to pee
only at scheduled recess times

safe sanctuary
for pitch-in lunches
assigned by grade level
donut Friday
to say "we made it"

comrades
sharing suggestions for
a better way to teach phonics
to a 4th grader who never got it
methods for dealing with that kid

who drives you nuts
a unique perspective from
others having the same "worries"
never feeling quite good enough

Nan Friedley

I Was Going to Clean the Bathroom, but Daredevil Happened

Blame it on NetFlix™…streaming
evil addiction…sucking me in
to watch shows I've
heard about but never seen.
Four seasons of *House of Cards*
and *Orange is the New Black*
thirteen episodes each season
total viewing hours…104…guilty
I've seen them all.

I never mean to do it
but one just melds into the next
with auto-play that counts
the number of seconds
until the next episode begins its
seductive summary hook inviting me
to stay for "just one more".

I might as well be cuffed
to the chair and ottoman
I promise myself to just watch two
but I'm a small-screen junkie.
Today I watched four episodes
back to back…only paused to pee.

For now I think I'm satisfied
but *Narco's* next season
was just released.

I'll just watch the first one.

Nan Friedley

Locked, Loaded, and Ready to Roll

Face washed, teeth brushed, contacts out, glasses on, jammies, ice water on the nightstand, ready for my favorite time of day…watching TV in bed. I usually fall asleep with it on, only to wake up in the middle of the night with that disturbing glow illuminating my bedroom.

I'd just crawled under the covers and predictable Rosie, my cat, sidles next to me for her nightly petting. Tonight's lead story on channel 7's eleven o'clock news is the probability of a magnitude 8 earthquake centered on the San Andreas fault. Cal Tech seismologists warn that a major earthquake is long overdue. I continue listening to this doom and gloom report on possible epicenter locations as I drift off to sleep.

A few hours later, I stagger to the bathroom to pee, crawl back into bed, locate the remote and turn off the blaring Friends rerun. Waiting for sleep to overtake me again I'm startled by a loud cracking sound that seems to emanate from under my bed. Rosie claws at the sheets as our mattress surf board rides the shock waves. Just when I think things can't get worse, my bedroom floor gives way.

As I'm freefalling into the earth's core, I recall accounts of near-death experiences. Will my whole life pass before my eyes? I anticipate scenes of high school band camp, college graduation, glimpses of dear friends and family played out in my personal surround-sound auditorium. Nothing. Out of the darkness, Diane my Allstate agent appears holding an unsigned earthquake insurance policy. *I warned you not to let this lapse.*

liz gonzález

Best Granddaughter

I
Years before surgeons
cut the lump
out of your trachea,
I promised vigilance
by your deathbed

My devotion in exchange
for you crying "Lichee, Lichee!"
nights after my father died when I was three
for stepping into his place
the times Mama let you
for giving me understanding
instead of scoldings

I should have known
I would never come through
When Grandma took afternoons off to shop,
I dreaded the simple responsibility
of boiling two weenies
and water for a steaming coffee cup
Your lunch stunk up the kitchen

"Television wastes the mind," you used to say
those days you wrote through mornings,
then stretched in a metal lawn chair
shaded by bougainvillea laced shadows
and read the daily Sun, classic novels,
the German version of LIFE

—always your hearing aid humming

During my summer breaks, you taught me
how to type, keep a personal budget—
even my one cent Bazooka bubble gum
had to be recorded,
play checkers and dominoes,
you assigned me to read the newspaper
and books in your glass door bookshelf
Too bad I wasn't interested
in your guitar and mandolin lessons

After your surgery,
on one of my infrequent visits,
I brought my VCR,
The Sound of Music, and *The Red Shoes*
The two movies you deemed important enough
to drive us granddaughters downtown to see

Nino dressed you in layers of clothes,
wrapped you in a blanket
to keep you from shivering
I hadn't considered
you had no energy to watch movies,
and rose only for me

I couldn't cross four feet of aqua carpet
to wipe the spittle dripping down your chin
To make up for it, I volunteered

to squeeze your two o'clock feeding
Impatience wasn't the reason
I pushed the plastic scented liquid
that prolonged your dying
into your belly too quickly,
jutting your spine,
your gasp
toward the ceiling

II
The Santa Fe whistle blew
quitting hour
when my tires snapped
your driveway gravel

It's a little over 60 miles
or an hour
from LA to Rialto
If I had left after Mama's call
I would have arrived before
the mortuary men rolled you away

"Now your grandpa will never
get to walk you down the aisle"
Grandma's front door greeting

III
I questioned my worthiness
to stand on the altar at your funeral mass
Mary Magdalene tainting
the family name
Upright at the jade marble pulpit,
zipped into a tailored dress,
your requirement

for family occasions,
I sucked the incense deep,
shared stories from the memoir
you typed on your Royal manual
Pages about your early years in the US,
before San Bernardino
and Grandma,
pages nobody knew about,
except me

Stepping off the train
at the Topeka depot in 1911
with your mother and little brothers
after a three day trip
from San Francisco del Rincon
to join your father,
moving to towns in Nebraska, Iowa,
Missouri, and Minnesota—
wherever your father could find work
The boxcar homes
The German Catholic school in Waterloo
and Thanksgiving turkey your mother "cooked
Mexican style with mole poblano,"
and your summer jobs—
water-boy, lantern-boy, farm hand,
helping your dad in the pool hall
The day you had to turn in your books
at Omaha Technical High School
where you played clarinet
in the orchestra and band
Your family needed your wages

Everyone in the church listened
Even the children stayed hushed

I looked over at the overpriced casket
Grandma insisted on
and imagined you smiling at me
like you did when you attended
all my school presentations

liz gonzález

Songs for First Dates

"Don't stand. Don't stand so close to me"
That boil on your neck
is as big as Frankenstein's bolts
and ready to burst
You could have covered it up
with a turtleneck
at least popped your collar
It's cold enough
No, I don't want spaghetti
with red sauce
Please don't order anything
creamy, red or white

"Don't stop believin'"
we're wrong for each other
for more reasons
than because I'm a shiksa,
like I told you
not to visit me at work,
like you insisted
on parking in the lot
and punctured your tires
when pulling into the exit,
like you're threatening
to sue my employer,
like after all that,
you expect me to go Dutch

"Please don't let me be misunderstood"

Just because it's Valentine's
Just because you gave me red roses
and a huge heart-shaped box of chocolates
Just because you bought me
an expensive steak dinner
I won't let you kiss me
Your father asked me
to go out with you,
give you a try
I did
Good night

"Don't stop me now"
Bubbles gurgle in my throat,
threaten to blurt a burp
as we french on my front porch
I waited so long for this date
How I wish
I never drank lemon lime soda
How I wish I could step inside
and let a loud gust loose
But I might wake up Mama
and our make out session will be over

"Don't let the sun go down on me"
Don't let this day end!
The summer hike
to Bonita falls in Lytle Creek
The cutest boy in high school
The joint of good stuff
His homemade picnic—
even brought a bottle of wine,
and plastic champagne glasses
The kiss sweet and refreshing

as our dip in the stream
We are on the uphill trail of adulthood
where the forest and desert collide
One of the best first dates of my life

liz gonzález

White Picket Fence House

All these years you fooled yourself,
thought your first home—
guarded by a white picket fence
your father built,
was the safe one

where you could sleep
through the night
without being touched,
where the sting of a belt
never bruised your skin

He died when you were three
Imagination filled
the few, windless
memories you have of life there:
rooms warmed by sunlight,

daddy rolling his chopper
into the back drive
Before you understood the reasons,
you sensed he had earned
a long stay in purgatory

Fifty-three years later you find out
he hit Mama in that house
You couldn't have slept through
nights he came home drunk
Now you know why Grandma said,

"Your father was not a good man"

Abah

Somehow the image of my father putting rice into the *ketupats*, on the eve of *Hari Raya*, kept playing in my mind tonight. The whole atmosphere, the feel, the sound, the smell, everything about it is so clear in my mind. *Hari Raya* songs blaring on the radio, Mak weaving the coconut leaves into *ketupats*, while Abah sitting by the doorstep in the kitchen, wearing only his *kain pelekat*, patiently putting rice into the *ketupats*. They would talk, argue, or simply piss each other off, as usual. My God, I really feel as if I'm back in kitchen with them now.

Everyone else in the house would just laugh at them, especially to Mak who simply had a lot to bitch about. "The house is messy and needs to be vacuumed. You still need to water the plants! And change the curtains. Oi, the cookie bottles are still not washed!" and on and on. But there was Abah, steadily and quietly putting rice into the *ketupats*, tied 6 pieces together into a bunch, and slowly put the bunch in a pot of boiling water. He was cool. He was drama free. No stress. He was just doing his task quietly, and looking forward to go to the mosque at dusk to hang out with his gang. That's my Abah. Coolest dude in town.

I miss him. I miss watching him fall asleep on the chair. I miss making fun of him. I miss laughing with him. I used to be so close to him when I was little. We were inseparable. In every get-together, party or wedding, I would sit with him. He and his friends were a lot more fun than my mother's. The men were noisier, more interesting, more raucous, and they laughed a lot more than the women. They were just fun.

When I was about 8 years old, I used to follow him

to Kuala Kubu Baru to run errands for his boss. That town was about 50 miles from home, so I'd get up early in the morning, get dressed in my school uniform, pack my lunch, and accompany him there. At about 11 am, we'd drive back home just in time for school. The afternoon school session usually started at 1 pm, so we had plenty of time.

Abah was the one who got me hooked on the Malaysian folktales. He'd buy a galore of books on Malaysian folktales so I could read in the car while waiting for him to do his thing. I devoured stories of the ungrateful son *Si Tanggang* who turned into a rock, that when a cruel king's fangs were thrown into the ocean, they turned into an island in *Raja Bersiong,* and that it is actually possible to acquire seven trays of hearts of mosquitoes in *Puteri Gunung Ledang*! So now, when I read stories on Malaysian folktales, I think of Abah and Kuala Kubu Baru.

We used to watch wrestling on the TV together. That man loved wrestling a lot. He'd get so animated that you'd think he's actually there, IN the ring! He sat criss-cross apple sauce on the floor in his *kain pelekat*, with me on his lap. We then watched wrestling with him screaming, jumping, cursing, and punching his fists at the TV. Haaaaaaaaa it was so much fun! I remember the feeling so well! It was like being in a bouncy house! Up and down, left and right, up and down! It was hilarious! I loved it!

Mak was sick plenty when I was young, so she was always in the hospital. For days and sometimes weeks. Abah would sneak me in at night, turning it into a fun adventure. Back then, the hospital guards were always Punjabi men wearing bright colored turbans. They had huge pointy mustache (I truly believe that mustache can literally poke someone's eyes blind, I swear), they were frightening and they had eyes in the back of their turbans. Swear to God. They could see and hear everything! But Abah always managed to sneak me in and sweet talk the nurses into letting us stay late. We had a great time, three of us hanging out on her bed talking, laughing, or playing Gin Rummy. Sometimes, the nurse would let us stay overnight. I slept on the hospital bed with my mother, and Abah on that plastic lounge chair. Fun fun memories. Jeez, I miss them tremendously.

So Abah pretty much took care of me when I was growing up. He woke me up for school, laid out my sharply ironed school uniform and spotless white shoes, and made me breakfast of his fabulous hot chocolate *Milo* and half boiled egg sprinkled with soy sauce and pepper. The egg was so delicious, boiled in perfect consistency, the best in the world I tell you. He also prepared my lunch consisting of rice, or bread with fried egg, and *air sirap*. He'd also give me 50 cents just in case I wanted to buy something else at the school canteen.

Abah was of course very protective of me. Five nights a week, I went to a religious class at the neighbor's house. Before class started at 7 pm, we had fun. We were children. We played tag, we climbed trees, we played jacks, we ran, we screamed, we laughed, we raced and we sweated. It was great! I had a pretty incredible childhood, I tell ya.

Anyway, there were several older girls who loved bullying by pinching us the little ones. These bitches were probably about two years older, not pretty, fat of course, and definitely were stinky. Of course.

One night I told Abah about it, and he got so mad that he wanted to beat the crap of these girls! He wanted to go to their houses that night! Seriously! Unfortunately and sadly, Mak said "Forget it. Let the kids handle it themselves." Damn, I would have enjoyed that. I would have savored every moment of them getting beaten up. So I told my sister Lin instead, who decided to pinch these bitches for me! The sight of them crying was beyond words. Delightful.

Oh, I have to tell this story. I was probably about 25

years old, and I was going through a party-till-dawn-every-night phase. One day, I got home at 3:30 am on a Tuesday. Yes, I was still living at home at 25. Being a Malay girl, you must live with your parents until you get married. I was a good girl. Haha! So anyhow, I quietly opened the door and tippy-toed into the dark living room. And boom, the light went on! There was my father, with a big stick in his hand, yelling "Where the hell have you been at this hour?" Oh My God, he scared the hell out of me.

Let's be clear. My father was a quiet man. He didn't talk very much. And he certainly was not a screaming man. Needless to say, that night ended my salsa hoopla in La Chivas.

Anyway, as I grew older, I wasn't as close to him anymore. I grew distant from him. I don't know why. The older I got, the harder it was for me to relate to him. I didn't know how and what to talk with him. Perhaps because I was his youngest. Abah was 53 years old when I was born, so I was his baby. He spoiled me rotten. Maybe he just wanted to me to be his baby forever.

I don't know. We simply grew apart, especially when I started working. It was hard. We didn't seem to have anything in common to talk about. I grew closer to Mak instead, it seemed easier to talk with her, or even to joke around with her. With Abah, somehow, I stopped getting him. I didn't know how to communicate with him.

He was still spoiling me though. Abah would send me and pick me from work, buy whatever food I wanted, he'd even wash my clothes! My God, he truly spoiled me and I was just ungrateful. Just thinking about it made me feel guilty because I know I was quite horrible. I took him for granted. Damn, I'm beginning to feel disgusted about myself now.

God, I miss him. I miss my father tremendously. He was a very good and loving father to me, even when I wasn't. I wished I had treated him better, talked to him more, and paid more attention to him. I wasn't mean. I just wasn't nice to him.

I didn't see him when he passed away. I didn't get to go to his funeral. I was here in California. I remember that night he died. I was in a restaurant, and my glass of ice tea just dropped on the floor. Pieces of glass everywhere. My first thought was, "I wonder who died?". That night, my brother-in-law called saying that he had some bad news. I almost fell because that I did not expect to hear that. I cried like hell. My Abah was gone and I couldn't see him anymore.

No one in the family, including Mak, was with him when he died. Apparently he went in for a nap, and he never got up. Everyone was home, but he just drifted off alone in the TV room. What a wonderful way to go. He was a cool and calm guy, and probably that's why it was easy and painless for him.

I dreamt of him two days after he passed away. He looked so good and so young, dressed in his favorite white t-shirt and baby blue with palm trees bermuda shorts. With a broad smile, he said, "Abah loves you, Ita. I have forgiven all your sins, so don't worry. I love you a lot." You have no idea how I felt when I got up that day. I cried and cried and cried.

It is still so clear in my head. The dream was so vivid. My family went through his stuff after he died and in his wallet, they found pictures of me. Only me. From baby pictures all the way to adulthood.

Anyway, I love you Abah. And I miss you. Especially when wrestling is on TV.

Glossary:
Abah – father
Mak – mother

Hari Raya – Eid El-Fitri, Muslim religious holiday celebrated at the end of fasting month

Ketupats – rice packed inside a container made from coconut leaves woven together

Kain pelikat – man-sarong

Air sirap – cold drink made out of rose-flavored cordial or syrup, sweetened with sugar

I am Green

Green green green. That's all that I love. I love the radiance and the peace it gives me. Looking at it brings a smile to my face. I flaunt the color shamelessly that everyone calls me the Green Camel.

Green is the color of serenity, fun, peace and whimsical. Natural yet complex. A combination of cool blue and sunny yellow. Boring blue and bright yellow. Exciting yet calm.

Green defines me. I am funny yet serious. I am friendly yet anti-social. I am an extrovert with my friends, but a complete introvert with strangers. I am open yet conservative. I am simple yet intricate. I am prudish yet freaky. I am boring yet exciting.

I bask in the city hubbub yet I savor my solitude at home. I love strutting in my high heels yet I feel very much at home in a boxing ring. I enjoy people yet I hate them.

I am Green. I am a mishmash of two opposites and two worlds. I am Complicated. I am a Woman.

Kamelyta Noor

Typical Muslim, am I?

Someone asked me today if I were a typical Muslim. And if it is difficult to be a Muslim. I said "I don't know. What do you mean by 'a typical Muslim'?" She just looked at me and shrugged. I started laughing.

I thought about it and I really thought about it. What exactly is a "typical" Muslim? And what exactly is "difficult"? Living as one, or merely living in America as a Muslim? Hmmm, that made me think.

I try to pray 5 times a day. I fast from sunrise to sunset during Ramadan. I give tithe to the poor. I believe that Allah is the one and only God, and Muhammad is the messenger of God. And someday, yeah, if I can afford it, I would like to perform pilgrimage to Mecca.

I think I am a good person. At least I try to be a good person, a good mother, and a good friend. Of course I scream at my kids, and yes, I do bitch about my friends and co-workers.

I cut coupons every Sunday. I buy grocery in stores with great sales. I check out Groupon and Living Social every week for fun deals.

I hate getting up in the morning to go to work. I dream of winning the lottery everyday so I don't have to go to work. I cook for my children, and I bring lunch to work every day.

I hate getting the mail because all I get are bills. I dream of winning the lottery everyday so I'm not scared of going to my mailbox. I enjoy reading the Avon book because I love their lipsticks and nail polishes. I surf the internet to read the latest news, but I especially look for gossips about celebrities.

I drive everywhere and I sing in my car. I curse at the drivers who goddamned drive 70 mph in a carpool lane. Come to think of it, I bloody curse at everyone anyway.

I can't sleep sometimes because I worry about my children, the bills, people, and sometimes work. I lay restless thinking about some Yahooos in my life, and how to deal with them.

I go to all my children's school events and I try to volunteer as much as I can. I curse when I get the fundraising packets. I read to my kids almost every night. I help Daniel with his homework and I teach Sadia how to bake cookies. Again, I dream of winning the lottery so I can be a stay-at-home mom with lots of shoes.

I bitch when my boss calls for a meeting 10 minutes before going home. I bitch when I see other co-workers screw around and get away with it.

So what exactly is a typical Muslim? How exactly am I supposed to be or live? What exactly am I supposed to do? You tell me.

Jane O'Shields-Hayner

Brook Hollow

The old house sat on a hilltop
At a fork in the rough dirt road.
Royalty and presidents had
Traveled up this trail, in its day.

A wild garden bloomed near the door,
And guests lounged, laughing, on its porch.
Mrs. A. was out on a walk
And Tom sipped his Jim Beam, rocking.

Down past the big barn and steep slope,
The creek poured over the edge of
A rock dam, where shining fishes
darted from shade into sunlight.

The dogs barked and circled a spot,
In the tall grass of the creek bed.
He walked down the hillside and looked,
And walked back up, cradling a fawn.

Many years later, I would ask
Why a man with loving kindness,
A man who saved the baby doe
Could not be trusted with my heart?

Treehouse Secrets

Vicki and I knew we were special. Her Dad built her a tree house where we could hide, share secret moments with our PBJ and baloney sandwiches, and devour comics from her bottomless collection. We learned a lot about life from  Peanuts, Superman, Wonder Woman, Tarzan, Archie, Dick Tracy, Homer the Ghost, Mickey Mouse, Dennis the Menace, and so many others. No matter the weather, we found ways to sneak up to that silent platform, sure that no one knew we were there. Television held little interest compared to our hideaway. Both of us were good students, though our parents were convinced our brains would rot from all of the visual trash we consumed. Their meager attempts to control our free time with other activities only increased the deliciousness of the private time we shared up in the trees. Daydreaming with my best friend really was special.

The summer of 1959 came crashing right into the middle of our simple life. Fifth grade ended on Friday the twelfth of June. Notebooks were stashed into the closest and out came the swimsuits, bicycles, and roller skates attached to old saddle shoes. We were all set for summertime and lazy days in the tree house sharing more secrets and dreams that were not to be shared with sisters. We lived on the military base at Ft. Bragg, North Carolina, because our fathers were career military officers. Our house bordered a large creek that meandered through a thick pine forest and harbored all sorts of wild animals including feral pigs and deer and coyotes. It was the pigs that scared us though because they crashed through those spindly pines in the evenings chasing us away from our crawdad fishing. The sultry humidity of June left us no choice but to seek the coolness of the table fan next to the kitchen door.

And then one still night our lives changed forever. A hooded stalker broke into the adjoined house and slashed my sister's best friend's head wide open. We locked ourselves up in the house and pulled the flimsy curtains over the old hinged windows, hoping the intruder would not push open those with broken cranks. My mother hovered endlessly while my father continued his work life.

We never found out if the villain was captured. My sister's girlfriend went away somewhere with her family. After three weeks of house captivity, all of our things were loaded into a moving van and we drove off in the old Chevy station wagon with sights set on our next life at Ft. Leavenworth, Kansas. And I lost track of Vicki.

Christine Pence

What's in my way?

I am in my way and
that is a pretty weak
statement. My days
pass with hours in
front of the computer
flashing words and
images and then
those needy students
who batter me with
questions and their

worries and their reasons why. And that brings me back to
being in my way. Where is the time I should be carving out
for me to find fulfillment in my own projects? I write and edit
and photograph and edit but the results are not yet satisfying.
Am I too critical or is it just my fear of rejection? My happy
almost seven-year-old grandson giggles over simple pleasures
every afternoon when I pick him up at school. He only asks
that I listen to him and pay attention to his questions and
questions and questions; and then that we take a few minutes
to play in the park. These precious moments fleet by but then
so does my life appear to be doing the same. I feel the pressure
of time and age getting in my way of enjoying the moments
and joys of learning new things. Tomorrow I must enter
another contest and tonight I must write another paragraph.
The student papers stack up waiting for me to grade, comment
and mostly to award gold stars so the writers can move to the
next class in their program. An email arrives with a happy note
from a happy student. My day is better already. My camera
fills the central spot on my desk right next to my computer,

reminding me that I really need a photo break to resource my creativity. Poets and Writers' latest magazine is under my camera, a purposeful location to keep me focused on words to accompany images and finding interested audiences.

Christine Pence

Ancillary and Peace

Now here's a challenge for my pre-dawn meditation hour today: reconciling Ancillary and Peace. This special time of the morning when I am not an ancillary to everyone else's priority to-do list and is my quiet peace time, I call my Ancillary Peace hour. Just saying the words in mantra style without any thought to the meaning bathes the precious moments with thoughts of harmony, tranquility, order, and calm– Ancillary Peace. "Peace be with you" as my religious friends often use to greet me, without any expectation of a response. Not unlike the casual greeting of the checker at Walmart "have a nice day" or of a passing acquaintance who has no real interest in my answer to "how are you." The order of the day, the peace, sets the tone for the inevitable crush of demands to provide ancillary support to my entourage. Am I really that necessary or is it simply easier for others to make demands of my time? Ancillary rolls out on the tongue without any of the Vulgar Latin trilling of "r" or is that because I am silently speaking in French and expect the guttural "r" to disturb the harmony? Ancillary life these days revolves around a schedule that is not my own. My morning hours are cut too short by obligations to collect others and to assure that their emotional, educational, physical, and intellectual needs are assuaged. The ancillary role demands me to be a specialist in life and growing up. And so I return to my morning mantra, Ancillary Peace, Ancillary Peace, Ancillary Peace. Ommm.

Suzanne Shimaya

The Camp

[This excerpt is from a longer work in progress]

Anne pressed her small upturned nose against the wire fence. The children near her screamed merrily in the background--playing a game of tag. A cold breeze whisked through her straight, short hair and her wool sweater, making her shiver.

"Come on!" one of her third grade classmates screamed. "Are you gonna play with us or not?"

Anne ignored the piercing voice and glanced around outside the Manzanar campgrounds. Mount Whitney looked beautiful in the distance--the sun glowed red and would soon set. It illuminated the grains of sand and dust that swirled with each gust of wind. Her eyes traveled over the California landscape made up mostly of cactus and tumbleweed. Once she thought she had seen a lizard scuttling across the sand and wanted to run outside the campgrounds to catch it, but she knew she would never be allowed to go outside--even if only for a little while.

She blew short breaths of warm air into her cupped hands. Then she made a game of poking her fingers through the square holes of the wire fence. Anne's older sister didn't like it when she played near the fence. Akiko said the top of the fence was a different kind of wire that would catch her hand, cut it, and make it bleed. Anne decided to only play with the wire holes closer to the ground.

Bored, she looked up at the tower that stood near one fence of the camp. When she first came here, she was amazed by it--she'd never seen a tower so tall before in her entire life! She smiled and waved to one of the uniformed men in the tower. He waved back; his large gun was slung over his broad shoulders. Anne thought about her cousin Amy's husband, James. He was in Europe fighting for the United States. Anne knew that Amy missed James because she slept with his picture by her side in bed. Anne heard her say that before she went to sleep she would hold the picture against her stomach while she talked to her baby growing inside her so that it would remain calm and know that the father was near, even if only a photo.

The same boy with the piercing voice screamed. "Are you gonna play in the game or not?" Anne looked away from the guard and at the boy. His body shook as he yelled, and he almost pitched forward and fell down. The other children roared. Anne knew he enjoyed being the class clown. She laughed at the boy.

Anne ran toward the children; though she ignored the boy because she found him silly, the prospect of running around excited her. After the game, she would eat her dinner in the mess hall, and go to bed later in her tar-papered home.

She often wondered when her father would return to her and her family. Her mother told her that he was in another camp somewhere across the United States. She hoped he had as many friends there for company as she had here in camp. But this thought left her as she joined in the game.

Later that evening, she and Akiko went to the mess hall to eat their dinner. As they pushed open the huge doors, Anne felt her stomach rumbling.

"Let's hurry," she urged her sister. As they both walked the noise from their shoes on the wood floor made clopping sounds that were regular and quick.

As they approached the end of the chow line, two small boys ran over and pushed their way forcefully in front of the two girls.

"Cut it out," Anne said, pushing one of the little

boys, causing him to stagger and grab onto the other boy for support. She hated those who cut in front of others in line.

The rude little boy made a menacing movement toward Anne. But seeing the bigger Akiko standing by, he checked himself and merely stuck out his pointed, red tongue at her.

"Ah, you're just an old stupid girl," he said. His eyes gleamed with defiance. "We got here first!"

Anne clenched her teeth so hard she thought a few of them would shatter under the pressure. She was about to push the little boy again when Akiko stopped her.

"Don't be stupid like them," Akiko said. Anne saw her frowned down at her before glancing around to see if anyone was bothered by the noise they had created. Akiko was raised not to cause any trouble, to be a good citizen, and to be polite at all times. Anne looked up to her big sister and did everything she said. She wanted to learn to be mature like Akiko.

Though Anne tried to contain herself, she couldn't help but feel angry. She felt her cheeks burn. In the middle of her body, an ache gnawed at her. But she kept quiet. The little boy in front of them laughed and whispered to his friend, who in turn looked around at Anne and giggled fiendishly.

To distract her thoughts, Anne looked down at the dusty, wood floor, and then around at the long rows of tables and wooden benches that filled the barrack. She saw two heaping stacks of sugared doughnuts and peanut butter cookies in the middle of each table, waiting invitingly.

These made her forget the mischievous boys, and her anger dissipated. She continued through the chow line with her sister.

They each carried a mess kit, composed of a tin plate, cup, and a fork. The handle was hinged to the side of the plate. Anne enjoyed snapping it up and down. She puffed out her cheeks and her chest and pretended to be a soldier; she envisioned the plate she was carrying as the American flag as she marched patriotically towards the front of the line.

Mr. Tanaka hovered over pots of steaming food. He was red-cheeked from the heat, and had on a white cloth hat that reminded Anne of the corner gas station attendants back home in West Los Angeles. Wrapped around his body was a thick white apron with food stains that looked like paint strategically placed on a blank canvas. She smiled as he ladled baked beans and Brussels sprouts onto the plates of the hungry individuals in line. Mr. Tanaka frowned and his face crinkled as he tried to avoid a face full of steam from the huge kettles.

As Anne approached, the smell overwhelmed her. She was as eager as the others to get her food. Her stomach was really beginning to protest its emptiness. "Here, Mr. Tanaka...." She stuck her plate out towards him. He did not talk to her but continued with his serving. Anne giggled as he puffed and grimaced.

Anne walked quickly towards her sister, letting a couple of Brussels sprouts roll around on her plate and mix in with the syrupy baked beans.

In order to reach Akiko, she had to walk down a crowded row. Most of the high school kids and parents in that row were huddled around their steaming plates. They talked quietly, or said nothing. The elementary and junior high school age children alone created the buzzing atmosphere in the huge barrack. Each row of tables and benches contained chattering and giggling children clanging their forks on their plates and their tins of milk on the tables.

Anne reached the table and sat down. As she and her sister ate, she watched Akiko who consumed her food methodically like an adult. First she ate the sprouts, then the beans, and then she drank the cold milk out of her tin cup with steady, continuous gulps.

In contrast Anne crammed her own small mouth with Brussels sprouts and beans. If she could have managed it, she would have added mouthfuls of the sugared doughnuts and peanut butter cookies.

At one point her older sister looked at her.

"You look like a chipmunk--can't you just eat your food without stuffing your mouth completely?"

Anne could only roll her eyes and give a muffled reply. A bit of a sprout popped out of her mouth. Akiko turned away and looked like she was pretending not to know her.

Anne lowered her head and continued chewing on the remnants of food. At one point, a bit of a bean skin got stuck between her two front teeth, and she stuck her index finger in her mouth in an attempt to dislodge it. Then she swiveled her finger around and tried to wiggle free a mixture of beans and sprouts that gathered in the back corner.

"Annie, don't do that," her older sister grimaced.

She immediately withdrew her finger, and instead used her tongue to reach the recesses in her mouth.

"You know, I'm only doing this for your own good," Akiko said in a softer tone, and patted Anne's head.

Anne quietly finished eating her meal.

Not long after dinner, Anne and Akiko walked to the shower facilities that were a couple of barracks away. The facilities consisted of a huge, drafty barrack, one side of which was rows of shower heads, faucet handles, and huge metal drains. On the other side, against the wall was a row of toilets. In the middle of that section were two rows of sinks back to back. Anne always used the shower area as quickly as she could; she felt funny whenever she saw all the naked bodies hovering around her. She would stare straight ahead at the shower faucet handles, and look at her face in the round, mirror-like knobs. Sometimes she would grin broadly into the shiny handles, giggling at the grotesqueness of her reflected features.

After showering Anne would use the toilet. It was difficult sitting there without feeling as if everyone was staring at you; there were no stalls, no doors. Anne tried to ignore the people around her whenever she used the toilet. The misery of not having any privacy made Anne think that camp life was a lot worse than school was back home.

"At least the bathrooms at school had stalls," she muttered to herself whenever she had to use the restroom, but as long as she finished with the showers and the toilets as quickly as possible, she was happy. And free to do anything else.

Judith Turian

Silence Spoken Here

Prologue

Really? Did I really sign up for this? Whatever was I thinking? It's in Big Sur, for heaven's sake. Well, that might be nice enough if it weren't for just a weekend—well, three days to be exact, and at least six-hours away. And in February? On a cliff above the ocean? It will probably be raining and cold, and as far as I can tell, the place doesn't have a comfy living area or meeting space to retreat to in sketchy weather or at night. So I'll be trapped in my room for three days with no one to talk to but God. And God can be difficult if He's into teaching you something or calling you to do some service. Especially when it's not something you really have any openness to learn or inclination to do. But, oh well. There's no one on the waiting list. And I committed to go.

So I prayed, "God, take away my anxiety and give me a sign." Just then, I opened my meditation book, and a poem by the Indian mystic Kabir appeared:

The Great Pilgrimage
I felt the need to go on a great pilgrimage
So I sat still for three days
And God came to me.

Hmmm. I wonder who put this little gem in front of my eyes?

My fear dissolved, and anticipation took its place. New Camaldoni Hermitage, here I come.

Quiet: On Arrival—Friday Night

So quiet. On entering my hermit's abode, I gasp in delighted surprise to find a wall of window overlooking the ocean at the far end of the room. Instead of the expected feeling of being closed in, I find myself drawn into a universe of infinite possibility. By the window, a door leads into a private garden, the ground covered in river rock, green shrubs under a leafless tree in the February late afternoon sun. Sitting in my little garden paradise, I feel life in the trees and movement in the ocean before I hear them. As I listen to the silence, the chirping of cicadas and the rhythmic roll of waves emerge as the symphonic soundtrack of silence. Sunset. Intense quiet, beauty and peace.

Night settles in, and my hermit's abode is a safe container. The beamed ceiling is a forest of wood. Smelling sweet, like a benign fire, rich with warmth, comfort, nurturing food for the soul.

Still: Morning—The First Day

The air is still, the woods are still, the ocean is still and so am I. Where have I ever felt such stillness? When?

Just now, I feel a light, gentle breeze blowing first on my neck, then swirling around me. It is the Holy Spirit. I know it is—kissing me, lifting me. I cannot pull myself away from this spot in my garden. If I walk away, I'm drawn back. No place has ever seemed so compelling. *Still*—a sacred word.

Freedom: Afternoon—The First Day

Unpaved trail of dirt and rocks, towering pines overlooking fields of wild pampas grass, feathery plumes swaying in the breeze. Sudden peeks at the ocean below and treetops highlighted by brilliant sunspots shining through dazzling blue skies.

When had adult life become so overwhelmingly busy with work, parenthood, aging parents, inward journeys of self-discovery and personal growth? How had I become so disconnected from the ability to be alone that I no longer spontaneously indulged myself in the pleasures of travel, spontaneous adventure and exploration? Afraid to be on my own, I no longer remembered that God and the present moment were enough.

Sitting at a picnic table, surrounded by woods and overlooking the ocean, I am aware that I am calmer, fuller, more centered, wiser, and healthier (though not younger—and I guess that's the point, isn't it?). I feel free to just be. At least for now, I am a human being, not a human doing or a human thinking. I don't need an assignment, a goal, or a direction. Can I carry this moment into the future, past the peace, beauty, safety and harmony of this place? Yes. Wherever I am, I can be free to stay or go, be alone at home or in nature, enjoying silence within or companionable peace with friends, follow the Spirit's call to walk down this forest path or explore that brilliant garden.

The intensity of the peace and stillness in this place at this moment is deep, embracing, encompassing.

Lost: Night—The First Day

Losing it. Time stretching out. Impatient with the quiet. Trying to pray, turning to scripture, attempting to read Barbara Brown Taylor's *An Altar in the World,* good solid down-to-earth spiritual advice. But I'm antsy and don't want to read even one more line of spiritual text. Pacing in circles on the gravel drive in front of my erstwhile peaceful, sacred abode. Rebellious! Overeating. Reading my novel. Am I undoing all that I had done?

At Vespers, monks chanting, incense burning, lights lowered. Centering Prayer. Praying for the fidgeting monk to find peace. I identify with him! Leaving before the meditation is done.

I am lost in goal orientation and expectations. I am lost in thoughts like, *What am I supposed to hear, find out, accomplish during this retreat?*

Found: Morning—The Second Day

Sitting in my garden drinking my morning coffee. A small bird with mostly blue feathers and white beak appears, hopping along, sometimes with lift off. This patch of grass, that seed, this branch of a tree, that fence post. Hop, hop, lift off. Look around. Hop over for a better view, lift off to a higher branch, then glide to fence post, hop some more. Check out the breakfast bowl. It has some good seeds, but the bowl is moved. No matter. Hop to its next patch of green grass, then off into the wild green and blue yonder!

That bird is living life on the grazing principle. Start off pecking or sunning at one spot in the garden, then hop to the next and fly to the next with no set plan. Just mindfully doing the next thing and covering a lot of ground. At the end of the day, it is fed, exercised, rested and relaxed.

Maybe I could learn from the little blue bird.
So what if I get up and leave the half hour of silence after Vespers before others do? So what if I read my novel? So what if

I drive down the hill, go into town and look around? Does that mean I broke connection with God and won't hear his voice? And that's the other thing—so what if I'm not being directed to hear, read, think about, pray about or talk about something? I think I'll go forward on this retreat living life on the grazing principle. Thank you, little blue bird.

Connection: Noon—The Second Day

Attention—The fruit of paying close attention is connection.

Walk. Sit. Gaze. Walk. Sit. Gaze. Every spot I sit is a snapshot, set up, positioned and framed perfectly. I see the wooden cross, a small crown of thorns placed delicately at the top, almost blending into the natural wall of brown hued rock to which it is attached. Then there are many viewpoints overlooking the craggy cliffs above the calm blue ocean. Or the fields of pampas waving in the light breeze and the old oak and pine trees on the forest path.

Each scene is quiet, yet speaking unspoken words. Still-- yet sending gentle ripples through my soul. Colorful, a palette of perfect, I mean PERFECT color with such depth, it draws in my eye, then my mind acknowledging it. My body relaxing and then I am gone, one with the set God has composed in nature to speak entirely and exclusively to me.

Reverence and Awe—Another way to connection.

A hawk flying in from the sea. Black and brown feathers against the unnaturally (or is this what is natural?) blue sky. Wide circles narrowing and coming closer. So close I can see the notches in its feathers, flapping up and down, controlling its height, glide, swoops, turns and swirls. Messenger of the gods in Native American lore, coming closer and closer so that it has me full in its glance. Focused vision. Right in front of me, its right eye deep black, zeroing in to let me know that I'm seen, not just noticed but seen and acknowledged. Then it dips its wing and flies away.

Truth: Sunset—The Second Day

What can be more true than the blue sky, the forest, the ocean, the ground we walk on, the sun rising and the sun setting, the dome of the heavens and the curvature of the earth?

This afternoon I sit down on a bench overlooking the ocean. The sun is in the sky, a ball of bright light, a brilliant spotlight shining across the water. The sunbeam spotlight flashes in a dazzling brightness that makes the fields of pampas feathers shine and shimmer in a translucent dance of white light. I sit transfixed. Colors appear across the horizon, orange at the bottom, then rose, then yellow. On the periphery of my vision, puffy pink clouds appear, billowing on the edge of the water and rising in a way that allows me to look through their great depth into the thinning air and eternity beyond.

On the horizon, a thin blue line outlines the curvature of the earth, a drawing of earth's gorgeous head, hair trained straight up, a crew cut colored with rose and orange and yellow. Hair on fire but not burning, just happily glowing.

I am drawn to watch this spectacle until night wins the day. Night is rising behind me, a dark scarf slowly covering the head of the world. I can't see the night or even sense it because the hairline above the face of the ocean is still in full color, though changing. The ocean turns to midnight blue, and the outline of the earth is deep blue-black. The sky above is still bathed in rose and yellow hues as the sunset begins to lower a grey veil. Strangely, between the yellow hair and the grey veil is blue sky—not midnight blue, but sky blue reminiscent of clear skies breaking through on a cloudy day.

Above and behind me, the sky is black and teaming with stars. The scarf being lifted over the head of the world is sparkling and shining with white stars, millions of them, the Big Dipper and the North Star leading the way.

Trees become black outlines against the midnight blue ocean. Devoid of color, but not shape, they look like shadow dancers, graceful and intricate against the rose, grey and blue of the sky and the darkening water of the ocean. Time seems to slow down, the last of the day wanting to hold on, refusing to yield to the black of the night. I watch transfixed as the starry scarf moves inexorably toward the hairline of earth's face, the horizon dividing the earth and the ocean from the sky and its stars. Still the night sky waits to make its final drop while the trees fade away, the ocean is lost and the firmament becomes all.

And to think that the sun is always rising and always setting somewhere in the world at every moment in time.

The Final Curtain: Monday morning

I wake to the last colors of sunrise facing west. Sitting in my garden on a breezy morning, thinking about all that I have seen and felt. How to capture the experience of stillness, freedom, connection and truth. How to capture the reverence and awe felt in the sunset as the ocean and land became the face of the earth and the slow steady raising of her starry scarf as earth covered herself with night. With Haiku.

Still, whispers Holy Spirit
She touches my soul
Offering freedom to be.

She speaks unspoken words
Gently rippling peace
Connecting body to soul.

Clearing mind, cascading Awe
Pine Tree cathedral
Embracing me in God's love.

Sunset, earth's hair on fire
Blue Ocean, Earth's face
Scarf of night slowly covers.

Peace, Be still
And know that I am God.

*Written at New Camaldoni Hermitage, Big Sur, CA.

Miracle Baby

When I was a little girl in pigtails, I asked my mother, "What is a miracle?" We were learning about miracles in our catechism class taught by the nuns at Sacred Heart church in Planada, California. Mother was a great storyteller and her favorite was the story of my birth, as it was indeed a miracle. According to her this is how I came to be.

In 1944, the 10th of December in Calera, Zacatecas, Mexico, the midwife said, "Mrs. De Landa you have a baby girl! She only weighs a pound. It is unlikely she will survive, as she did not cry at birth because her lungs are not fully developed."

The midwife was instructed to continue. My umbilical cord was cut and tied. I was bathed then given to mother to breastfeed. But there was a problem; my mouth was too small for one to nurse. So I was fed with a medicine dropper. I was wrapped in a "rebozo", which is the Spanish word for shawl. I was soothed and comforted by the warmth of Mother's body and the beating of her heart.

There were no incubators. Mother had to make her own heating elements, warm water bottles to keep me from becoming chilled. Keeping me warm was of major concern. I was given a bassinet among the many gifts that arrived daily when word spread a one pound baby was born. The bassinet was too big. I was placed in a shoebox on top of the mantle on the fireplace in our adobe house Father had built on Cinco de Mayo Street.

On the third day, even though I began to cry, I was not thriving. My parents drove to the nearest town to see a physician. After examining me he told them, "She will not survive - too small." My mother feeling desperate, asked the doctor to prescribe something to help me. He instructed her to boil white rice, strain it, and give me only the water from the rice. She followed the doctors' orders and before anyone knew it, I was gaining weight.

My parents remained positive. Not only did I survive, but by six months, I spoke a few words and startled my parents. At nine months, I stood up and began walking. They were elated. Time moved quickly and soon I began running and jumping with my brothers and sisters. There was no indication that I had been born two months early. I was growing and thriving.

Through my mother's determination and resourcefulness and my father's strength, I beat the odds. It amazes me that I survived without an incubator, specialized nurses, pediatricians, and all the modern neonatal conveniences involved with babies of today. What a miracle!

Circle of Life

Circle of life—
the sun luminous,
the moon iridescent,
the earth spinning ball,
the season sequential life circles—
a mystery beginning with birth
childhood, adulthood, old age,
and then the end. Another
life born taking place
of the one that left.

Gudelia Vaden

Ode to a Button

Oh little brass button
So round and shiny
You've held up my britches that covered my hiney
But as years go by
Your brilliant brass has come to pass
You've been kept in an old button jar
Until someday when something comes undone
And I'll need you to cover my bum

Gudelia Vaden

Natalie, My Daughter

Teaches children critical thinking skills.
Does 1 + 1 = 1?
Her method is exponential,
a lifelong learning pursuit.

Gudelia Vaden

The House That Dad Built

From his brow and sweat,
My dad built a house
of mud, straw and assorted bricks.

His pride and joy (no doubt),
a place of accolades and nurturing.
Best adobe house of all.

Gudelia Vaden

When Gudelia Met Tom

One clear day in April, when the sun was shining, the birds were singing and Riverside smelled of orange blossoms. My granddaughter, Natasha, asked me, "How did you and grandpa meet?" Even though it has been fifty years, I will always remember the day we fell in love.

In the spring of 1964, I was nineteen years old and Tom was twenty-four. We were students at Merced College in Central California. The campus had not been built so the classes were held at the Merced County Fairgrounds. As I went from class to class I had memories of the fair where livestock, pieces of art work, crafts, pies and preserves were judged. Once I entered mother's doilies and they won a blue ribbon. It seems like it was just yesterday, that Tom and I munched on buttered corn on a stick. What a delight it was to ride the Ferris wheel! Having the classes at the fairgrounds was fun and it took the stuffiness out of going to college.

I took basic education courses and Tom took math classes. He even carried a slide rule with a leather holder, which was the equivalency of today's calculator. I did not know it then, but it was the beginning of life in the makings of a mathematician, a career he pursued with dedication and skill.

Life was not all study and no play. There were breaks between classes. Though we had no classes together, we met at the ice cream vending machine. I put my two coins into the machine and as I reached down to grab my ice cream bar, I looked up and our eyes seemed to lock. For a couple of minutes, we gazed into each other's eyes. He was wearing a bright red shirt with buttons down the front. I had never seen such beautiful green eyes on a man. His eyes were reflecting the red shirt; it appeared as if he had red sparkles of light in his eyes. I thought to myself, is red really his color? His blond hair was sun bleached and almost white. He had a big toothy grin, sort of shy, but one of confidence and strength. He was wearing blue and black plaid Bermuda shorts. He had the most gorgeous legs I had ever seen. They were muscular and toned. He humbly spoke of having been stationed at Lowry Air Force Base in Colorado and that he had skated with Peggy Fleming. While we were eating ice cream and chatting, we seemed to connect. I believe it was love at first sight.

Soon after we met, Tom asked me out on a date to the A and W drive-in for a hamburger and shake. We sat in his white pearl Austin Healy sports car and a short skirted carhop in roller skates took our order and brought it on a tray that hooked to the window of the car. We were encouraged to remain seated until we finished eating. Eating out made dating so much fun!

One year later, during spring break, Tom asked me out to Yosemite National Park, which was about a one and a half hour drive from my home. My parents had rules and one was that I could not date far away from home. The thought of asking my strict parents for permission to go on this outing sent chills down my spine. My cousin Rudy was in a calculus class with Tom. Rudy made friends with Tom. He went home and told my aunt that Tom was going with me and he was the nicest young man on campus, and that he was also excellent at math. The rumor about Tom travelled fast, so when I asked my dad if I could go, he told me he had heard good things about Tom and he let me go.

Yosemite is beautiful in the spring. I could see the pine trees sending down their aromatic and luscious scents. The birds were blending in with the trees and bushes. This is when he proposed to me, amid the beautiful wild flowers that were everywhere and the cascading waterfalls that were among us. Water was trickling down a creek and it looked so clear. I could see his reflection and mine in the water, as if waiting for an answer to a proposal. I felt like my breath was taken away, as I could not speak. The beauty of Yosemite put me in a trance, as well as the proposal. It was too overwhelming and unexpected. This is where he showered me with kisses and many more after that. I looked into his green eyes, that were almost emerald, but more like teal green mixed with zap green, as when an artist mixes colors to find the exact one. I finally said, "Yes, I will marry you." I knew he was the right one for me.

I told my parents that I was going to marry Tom and they gave us their blessing. He was an airman with the Air Force, and we could get shipped anywhere. There was talk that we could be sent to North Dakota. My older sister, Socorro, planned my wedding. She was as excited as I was and had never planned one before. At twenty-one years of age, I was the first one of my two other sisters to get married.

We were married on January 22, 1966 at Castle Air Force Base chapel in Merced, California. The weather was sunny with beautiful blue skies and warm weather. I wore an ivory colored floor length gown made of satin and adorned with miniature pearls throughout the dress and train. My veil was short and transparent. My best friend Zozima was my maid of honor and my two sisters, Socoro and Elisa, were my bridesmaids. They all looked lovely in their royal blue silk dresses. My four year old niece, Debbie, was the flower girl and her older brother Philip was the ring bearer. After the priest declared us man and wife, we kissed and were ready to go to the reception. My mom and aunt Reyna made enchiladas, chicken and various salads. The three tier cake was white with little blue roses and a bride and groom on top. My older sister made the fruit punch and a cousin spiked it with tequila.

We left the reception early to go on our honeymoon for a month, travelling in a 1966 red Volkswagen bug filled to the brim with wedding gifts and all of our belongings. We started out with the Grand Canyon and ended our trip in Grand Forks, North Dakota, where the weather was 40 degrees below zero. We survived the great blizzard of 1966, the great spring floods and the lightning storms in the summer.

I had never been out of California before and made it through very extreme weather conditions. Our warmth and love for each other made it possible. While it was freezing outside, we were sizzling inside. It makes me wonder if we were blessed by God to be one because it was and has been for fifty wonderful years.

Thomas J. Vaden

Blueberry Hill

A dust patch sat just off the highway 99 with a café and a gas station, and 18 wheelers parked in random patterns. At first glance, it was scary looking, almost like an ancient abandoned fortress with vertical stone walls seemingly made of the available stones found nearby. A foreboding dilapidated wood fence enclosed the flat roof. The setting sun shed an eerie glow over the scene as the fading light cast dancing shadows across the rocks. Large weathered neon signs mounted high up on telephone-pole stilts punctuate the dim sky with eerie sinister red and blue glows. "Blueberry Hill" and "Café" lights beckon weary highway travelers to enter the grounds and a neon arrow points the way. An oversized billboard sits atop the front entrance. Another smaller neon sign lights up the entryway with the word Café.

Delia, my girlfriend and I, were just returning from a terrific weekend ski-trip at Tahoe on an old dark blue Air Force bus, when a sudden shuddering shook the bus, shattering our peaceful ride. The bus had to pull off the road quickly. To our dismay, we came to rest on this ominous patch of dust on the outskirts of Livingston. We were in a panic state as it was getting late. The Air Force bus needed the tires replaced and the tires would have to be sent from Castle Air Force Base, about 50 miles away. The tires, however, would not be sent until the morning. If we stayed, we would have to either sleep on the bus, or stay up all night, dining at this weird Blueberry Hill café. This was her first long weekend trip away from home and her dad would be extremely worried if we did not make it back in time.

God, I have mixed emotions. I would certainly like to spend the night and another day with my girlfriend. But I was afraid that if I didn't get her home on time, I would be in deep trouble with her dad. After all, he was very protective of his daughter. Everyone knew he carried a pistol and he knew how to use it. I gave up on my amorous thoughts and decided that we should call home with an explanation of the situation. But, we had no way to call if we stayed on the bus. Hungry and desperate we knew what we had to do. What could we lose? So we left the sanctuary of the bus and took our chances on this mysterious Café. After all, truck drivers had the reputation of only eating at the best places on the road. While dining at the Café, the Fats Domino baritone voice was spinning in my head:

> *I found my thrill*
> *on Blueberry Hill*
> *On Blueberry Hill*
> *when I found you …*

Of course, I flipped through the pages of the mini Juke box at our table, found Blueberry Hill and listened to the lyrics. The lyrics matched my feelings at the time. I finally got up enough nerve to place the dreaded phone call. But, as soon as I heard her father's voice, big brave me chickened out, and I quickly shoved the phone into Delia's hand. You talk to him I pleaded. She sighed, told him our situation and asked if he would come and pick us up. He said he would but it would take him several hours. We spent that time drinking coffee, eating scrambled eggs and sharing a delicious blueberry pie.

We talked about how just 30 years before our dilemma, there must have been a luscious blueberry farm just off a winding two lane road passing through a place in the sticks in the San Joaquin Valley that would someday be called Livingston. A two lane divided highway was then built and a farmer's blueberry stand likely appeared at the side of the highway, destined to become the Blueberry Hill Café.

Today, 50 years later, the little café at the outskirts of Livingston no longer exists. The only memory is an isolated black and white photo in the historical archives of Merced County. Highway 99 now crosses over the dust patch once called Blueberry Hill. One cannot even see Livingston from the freeway; however, it's still there on the map. I may not know or remember much about Livingston, but I will always remember our night in the Blueberry Hill Café. I married Delia about a year later. Today, we are still together after 50 years of wonderful memories.

Thomas J. Vaden

The Yin and Yang of Wasted

Was my youth wasted or did my youth prepare me for the future?
Was my youth wasted or did I enjoy my youth?
What is the meaning of wasted?

If I do not love what I do but do it greatly, have I wasted my youth?
If I love what I do but do it poorly, have I wasted my youth?
What is the meaning of wasted?

Is wasted measured by what one has accomplished or by what one
has enjoyed?
Is wasted judged by others or by oneself?
What is the meaning of wasted?

Can one achieve great things in life but others feel that one's life has
been wasted?
Can one achieve nothing in life but others feel that one's life has not
been wasted?
Who determines if one's life was wasted?

If I do not love what I do and have achieved nothing,
almost all would agree that my life was wasted.

If I love what I do and have achieved great things,
almost all would agree that my life was not wasted.

I believe that I love what I do.
I believe that I have achieved great things.
Most assuredly, all must agree that my youth was not wasted.

Life at Ten

My dad left us -I did not know
What happens next -a world so cold?
My mom alone
With five at home

Orphanages would take only two or three
Problematic solutions not to be
Grandma steps in
Life starts again
A blessing forever
Kept family together

My grandma a disciplinarian
My grandpa a spoilitarian
Little I knew lessons learned then
Would revisit me once again

Granddaughter moved in with us
    Without warning
    A little disarming

What do I do now?
    Be like my grandma?
    Be like my grandpa?

Shall I discipline?
    Discipline needed
    But never heeded
    Trials and tribulations
    Heart with palpitations

Shall I spoil?
  My life calmer
  Her life simpler
  Life goes on
  Tribulations be gone

Thomas J. Vaden

Light Bends (Tanka)

The moon shines brightly
Einstein researching the stars
The mind shines brightly
The moon eclipsed by the earth
Brilliant concept verified

Frances J. Vasquez

Capirotada

Family, Love, Tradition, and Unity

My family loves Capirotada - a traditional bread pudding-like dessert popular in México. My mother inspired me to appreciate it when I was a child growing up on Church Street in Highgrove. It holds multi-layers of significance, beyond the culinary delight and sustenance it provides. I have fond memories of Mamá making Capirotada every year during the 40-day season of Lent that begins on Ash Wednesday and culminates on Easter Sunday. It was a popular casserole dish that most Mexican families in my neighborhood served on meat-less Fridays. The layered bread-cheese-nut-fruit casserole provided ample protein and other nutrients to the religious fasting diet. Devout Catholic families such as ours were steadfast about observing the then-strict fasting rules during this annual period of abstinence, penance, and sacrifice.

I lovingly make Capirotada once a year on the evening of *Sábado de Gloria*. Over the decades, it has become my signature dish to serve at our family's annual Easter Sunday celebration at Armida and Ray's spacious home on Horace and Hawarden Drive in Riverside. I'm expected to bring it. No one else in our extended family prepares this traditional Mexican concoction. My Capirotada is served as dessert during the afterglow of our scrumptious Easter supper. We appreciate how the diverse ingredients and flavors blend and mix incredibly well together. The variety of the ingredients complement each other. The subtlety of the spices add complexity to the dessert, and the flavor improves with time. Like bread pudding, people either love Capirotada or they dislike it. No equivocation about this dish. High-quality, authentic ingredients and conscientious preparation matter.

There are regional and family variations in Capirotada recipes and in its manner of preparation. Like my Mamá, I initially began by using the basic ingredients: day-old French bread, Monterey Jack cheese, peanuts and raisins. The diverse, yet complementary mixture of food items are layered together to make a delectable casserole. Later, inspired by Lucille's popular recipe at the long-gone Enrique's Restaurant in downtown Riverside, I started to incorporate diced fresh apples and slivered raw almonds instead of peanuts.

With the passage of time, I became more experimental, more authentic with my choice of ingredients. I prepare an aromatic syrup using *piloncillo* (raw cane sugar cones), *canela*, whole cloves, and water. I deftly layer the components in a large *cazuela* or baking dish. I liberally drizzle the rich syrup over the Capirotada mixture and bake in an oven until the dish is bubbly and golden brown. The key to a delicious, moist Capirotada is in the richness and generosity of the syrup. Not enough syrup and the concoction comes out dry and tastes like plain corn flakes. My family prefers our Capirotada prepared with liberal portions of fresh and dried fruits, almonds, and lots of syrup.

The Easter 2016 Capirotada that I prepared was a slight variation of my 105-year old Tía Cuca's recipe from Providencia, Sonora. For the first time, I added fresh diced *platano macho* (plantain banana), and cubed candied *biznaga* (Sonoran Desert cactus) that I brought with me from a trip to Sonora in February. By all accounts, the Sonora-style Capirotada was the best I've ever made. Tía Cuca uses buttered, toasted *pan birote* instead of French bread. She begins by lining the *cazuela* with flour tortillas, then adds layers of diced *platano macho, queso fresco ranchero* (crumbled fresh Mexican cheese), dried prunes, raisins, peanuts, and cubes of candied *biznaga*. She adds fresh orange peels to her simmering syrup of cinnamon and cloves. A unique touch, Tía Cuca crowns her Capirotada with a *turrón,* an egg-white meringue just before baking. Some day, I hope to prepare a turrón crowned Capirotada in honor of my favorite aunt from México.

Mitla Café on Mt. Vernon Avenue in San Bernardino makes a moist, flavorful and authentic Capirotada that is as good as homemade. They serve it exclusively on Fridays during Lent. They too, serve it as dessert to culminate their special Lenten fare of *Tortas de Camarón con Nopalitos en Chile Colorado.* Gastronomical Heaven! My friends and I enjoy dining at Mitla Café during Lent to partake of this delectable comfort food that connotes nostalgia, *amor, y aveses, trístes momentos de la vida.* Capirotada is akin to a long-time loyal friend whom you love dearly and whose enduring friendship you savor as time goes by.

One January evening while I was out shopping for groceries after work, my grandson Oscar amazed me when he called on my mobile phone to say he wanted to make Capirotada for a high school Spanish class project. He said he needed my help. His choice of topic almost floored me. He asked me to help him prepare it, because the project required family involvement. "But Mijo", I replied, "it's not even Easter season. Let's make something else that's more appropriate for the season. Like buñuelos or empanadas," I added. But, Oscar asserted, "No, I want to do my project on Capirotada." He quickly implored, "Besides, Nana, you're the only person I know who makes Capirotada." Seeing that Oscar would not be swayed, I readily consented and replied, "Yes, of course, Mijo. I'll be glad to help with your project."

It was difficult for me to fathom. I kept thinking, *Oscar? Quiet, wrestling jock, Oscar! He had never before indicated that he even liked Capirotada. It's often said, you have to watch out for the quiet ones.* Como dice el dicho, "Mosca muerta". Usually, it's the family elders who rave about my Capirotada. Every year, they look forward to enjoying a portion for dessert on Easter evening, or to take home a coveted *bocado* for the next day. It pleased me to know that from a large array of topics to select from, my teenage grandson chose my signature Lenten dish for his Spanish Class Familia Project.

I wrote down a shopping list of ingredients for my son Andrew (Oscar's dad) to purchase for the project, except I took my own genuine canela sticks and whole cloves. Authentic Mexican cooks use *canela*, true cinnamon (*Cinnamomomum Zeylandianicum*) which imparts a subtle spicy flavor. The *canela* bark is formed with concentric layers that splinter easily when the sticks are broken. The brown bark is softer and thinner than cinnamon from the Cassia tree, whose sticks are hard and reddish brown in color. In México, most Capirotada recipes call for peanuts. They impart a delicious earthy flavor. Peanuts taste best when the Capirotada is consumed immediately, because they become rubbery in the casserole after more than a day. Almonds, however, retain their crunchy texture and still taste great over time.

On the Sunday afternoon before Oscar's project was due, I went to their home to demonstrate and work with Oscar on preparing the Capirotada. We took photographs to document each step of the process for his research paper. While the Capirotada baked in the oven, Andrew went to Rite-Aid to have the photos reproduced for Oscar's report. Meanwhile, I accompanied Oscar to his room to read on the computer screen the research paper he had written on the origins of Capirotada. He surprised me again with how thoroughly researched and informative the paper appeared. I learned that Capirotada originated in Spain! Not in México as I had presumed.

Oscar wrote that centuries ago, the Spanish missionaries brought the recipe to our Continent. Because the dish is served primarily during Lent, each major component has a special significance relating to the Passion of Christ.

The bread represents the body of Jesus. The cinnamon sticks correspond to the wooden Cross. The cloves signify the nails of the crucifixion, and the syrup represents the blood of Christ. Previously, I had no idea of the Christian symbolism of Capirotada. I learned so much from reading Oscar's report. I ventured into a journey of discovery that melds Spanish religious and culinary traditions with indigenous Mexican culture, both on historical and familial levels. Too often, it seems, we take for granted the simple, enjoyable things in life without reflecting on their historical context. To be sure, when we teach, we learn. Oh, the cycle of life is wonderful. It was edifying to assist my grandson with this high school class project, and gain knowledge of the fascinating bicultural and religious origins of Capirotada.

On the following Monday morning at Spanish class, Oscar served his classmates sample-size portions of Capirotada that my daughter-in-law had prepared in individual paper baking cups. With enthusiasm and a bright smile, he presented an oral report on his project. My heart jumped with joy to listen to Oscar recount that he began his narrative by stating animatedly, "My Nana has been making Capirotada every Easter for over thirty years...." When Oscar shared with me how affirming his Spanish class presentation was received, I smiled widely and my eyes sparkled with pride - like a cacklin' hen - *como una gallina cluéca*. Oh, the cycle of life is wonderful. It was particularly edifying to assist my grandson with this high school class project, and gain knowledge of the interesting bicultural and religious origins of Capirotada.

One of the benefits of reading Oscar's research paper is that I no longer discard the cooked cinnamon sticks after the syrup is completed. I now save the pieces to form a decorative cross as a garnish on top of the Capirotada. A significant aspect of Oscar's Capirotada project is the fact that he noticed and paid attention to our family's cultural and culinary heritage, and traditions. It impressed me that this relatively obscure cuisine was relevant to my adolescent grandson. This was affirmation that Oscar got it. He understood that family traditions matter - as do the generous allocation of love and attention we share and impart with one another.

One November day, the then-Poet Laureate of the State of California, Juan Felipe Herrera led an impromptu-style poetry reading on the Main Street Peace Walk near the Gandhi statue in downtown Riverside. There gathered: retirees, UCR students, government office workers, shoppers, Inlandians of all stripes and of diverse cultures. Juan Felipe implored upon us to value our ancestors' stories. Value our parents' and grandparents' stories, he beckoned. "Value your own stories, and most of all, your voices... celebrate your voice when you make enchiladas and tamales. Celebrate your beautiful voices. Share your voices," he intoned. To conclude his amazing "guerilla" unity poem performance, Juan Felipe asked everyone present to come up with one word on unity. And with our own voice, he said, "shout out one word, *una palabra* that comes out of your heart." To Juan Felipe's count of three, I raised my voice and shouted with glee, "Capirotada!" After the performance, I shared with him the story of Oscar's Spanish class project. Juan Felipe insisted that I write the story just like I had told it to him.

In the spirit of gratitude and unity, I'm also sharing my celebrated Capirotada recipe with this story. Gracias Mamá y Tía Cuca. Thank you, sage poet. And, a special appreciation to Oscar for valuing our family traditions. There is an old Mexican *dicho* that says: "Como una Capirotada bien hecha". The saying connotes "Job well done with a complex, diverse mixture."

* * *

This personal essay was inspired by a writing prompt led by Minda Reves during an Inlandia Institute Summer Boot Camp "Gateway to Memoir" workshop. I revised it during an Inlandia Creative Writing Workshop led by Jo Scott-Coe. Juan Felipe Herrera encouraged me to write about Oscar's Capirotada project during a "Unity" poetry event in downtown Riverside while he was California State Poet Laureate. Juan Felipe is the current Poet Laureate of the United States. Thank you, esteemed writing mentors!

Nana's Capirotada Recipe

Ingredients:
1 Loaf of French Bread (day old)
1/2 Lb. Monterey Jack Cheese
1 Cup Slivered Almonds
3-4 Apples (Granny Smith or Macintosh)
1 Cup Raisins
1/2 Cup Butter
2 *Canela*/Cinnamon Sticks
3-4 Whole Cloves
1 Qt. Water
3 or 4 *Piloncillo* Cones (or 2 Cups Brown Sugar)
Pinch of Salt
Preparation:

Syrup: place water and piloncillo in a large sauce pan and add a pinch of salt. Bring the water to a soft boil and simmer until the piloncillo has melted; add the canela sticks and whole cloves and simmer gently until syrupy (approximately one hour). Strain the syrup before drizzling it onto the casserole.

Bread: pre-heat oven, 350 degrees; slice the bread and place on a baking sheet to toast on both sides in a hot oven until golden brown. Slice or tear the bread into bite-size pieces and set aside.

Peel and slice the apples thinly into a bowl; grate the cheese into a bowl. Generously spread butter on an oblong 9 X 13-inch glass baking dish. Place a layer of bread evenly on the bottom of the baking dish. Cover the bread with a layer of apple slices, then sprinkle with raisins, grated cheese, and slivered almonds. Repeat the layers until the dish is full. It is best to apply almonds as the top layer for a crunchy texture. Slowly drizzle the strained syrup all over, taking care to saturate the entire casserole; finally, dot the top with the remaining butter.

Cover the dish with aluminum foil and bake in a pre-heated oven, 325 degrees for 35-45 minutes until bubbly. Remove the foil during the last 10-15 minutes to brown the top. Let cool and serve warm, or refrigerate to serve cold. Capirotada is delicious left-over fare. Like many casseroles, the subtle flavors of the intermingled ingredients improve after a few days.

Helpful hints:
Traditional recipes use *bolillos/pan birote*, small oval bread rolls (similar to baguettes) popular in México and in California. Cut 6 rolls in half (lengthwise) and toast on both sides.

Piloncillo, bolillos, platano macho, and *canela* are readily available in markets specializing in Latino products, like Cardenas or el Super. Stater Bros also carries these ingredients.

Buen Provecho ~ Enjoy!

Mae Wagner

Overbooked

The summer of 2016 has been unbearably hot and the first day of August was no exception. This was the day of my husband Alex's three-month appointment for an infusion at the oncology department at Kaiser Permanente in Riverside.

Each time we go, all twelve or fifteen reclining chairs in the treatment room are filled; most patients are receiving chemo. Next to each recliner, there is a medicine tree holding two or three bags of fluid that drip, drip, drip into a vein in the patients' arms.

I have been to these rooms before. Once with my young niece in Mandan, North Dakota who was being treated for aggressive breast cancer and also with my daughter who has chronic lymphocytic leukemia. Fortunately, her CLL has not advanced; her treatment thus far consists of infusions of iron dextrose in an effort to help her red blood cells in their battle against the prolific white cells.

Many of the patients in Kaiser's Riverside facility have the routine down pat. They bring reading material, drinks and food. They know they are going to be there for a while. Some sleep. Most are accompanied by another person. Some, sadly, are not.

On this day, they have overbooked the infusion room. People are waiting for an available recliner—but when the average appointment lasts four hours or more, they don't empty quickly. There is no chair for my husband; his nurse—who tells us the overbooking is becoming increasingly common—puts us in a crowded, claustrophobic exam room that seems to be a dumping ground for various equipment.

The male nurse tells my husband his veins are small

and fragile but he manages to get the port into his arm. Then we wait while the pharmacy mixes the particular potion that goes into the bag connected to the plastic tube feeding into Alex's arm. I ask him how he is doing and he says he is really hungry and is thinking of a grinder from Delia's. Today he decides he will ask for double meat on his. He thinks he will have capicola for a change.

Delia's, a long-time restaurant on University Avenue in Riverside, is our go-to reward after his oncology appointments. I've been a fan since the mid-fifties and Alex used to take his family there years ago as well. We reconnected after being neighbors forty-some years ago and have been married for nearly seven years. I go with him to all of his appointments—and, believe me, there are many.

Soon, he is finished and we are on our way. But I can't help but think of all of the brave people everywhere, sitting in similar recliners, covered with warm blankets and hooked up to otherwise dangerous ingredients concocted into a medical stew of medicine that they hope gives them a few more days, months, weeks and years.

Alex often says, "If we can go to the moon, why can't we cure cancer?" I have no answer.

We go about our daily lives, not even aware of the many battles that are being fought on a daily basis in rooms like this. This is just one treatment room in one facility in one city on one Monday. There are places like this all over the city, all over the country, all over the world.

Yes, we are unaware, not even thinking about it—until there we are, in a room like this ourselves.

And now, on to Delia's for our grinders—ham for me, double capicola for him.

And life goes on. At least for now.

Mae Wagner

Downtown

Sitting in front of the library
watching the people
as the sun sets behind me in the west.
I hear the cloppety clop clop of women's high high heels
before they come into view—and I wince
knowing their feet have got to be hurting and the price they may pay
when their feet are old and tired and bunionated

The couple on the porch of the Unitarian Church—
did they just kiss?
Are they really a couple
or just two lost souls
trying to make a connection?
Wait—did he just toss a piece of trash?
How dare he litter this hospitable place?
A church next to a library
is a draw for the homeless—at least, they look homeless
while others pass by, all dressed up
heading for some fancy event
at the Mission Inn.

I hear the roar and pop pop pop of a motorcycle
passing behind me
while in front of me
some ride by on bicycles
silently circling around and through the walkways of the library.
 Others are on foot
or sitting on the hospitable library lawn
feeling like this is a belonging

kind of place
right here within the heart of Riverside
a city I have long loved.
Church bells chime
On the hour and half hour.
Funny how quickly time slips away
sitting in front of the library
waiting for the workshop.

Mae Wagner

Zack

Twenty-five years ago
on April 22, Earth Day
fittingly enough
a day already honored
by my daughter
who allowed me to be present
for this amazing process of birth.
She gave a final push
and a new little person
came into this world.
And now,
twenty-five years later
his own child
is growing in the womb
of the woman he loves.
I want to believe that
the efforts we make
in honor of Earth Day
will mean this new generation
and those to follow
will still have an Earth
on which to celebrate this day.

Mae Wagner

Cats and Dogs

I've always been more of a dog person than a cat person—not that you have to be one or the other—but cats are different. I once read that you don't own a cat—it owns you.

When my sister, Betty, and I were growing up in North Dakota, we always seemed to have pets like our dog Cricket or our cat, Tiger. Betty loved that orange striped tabby. She had—and still does—such a tender heart and she wanted to treat that cat like a baby. She would even wipe Tiger's nose.

One year, Santa brought us a blue doll buggy—which I have to this day. I remember the time Betty dressed Tiger in my brother Stan's white baby dress and put him in the buggy.

Well, Tiger was having none of that. He leaped out of the buggy and sprinted for the only tree in our huge yard—and up he went, dress and all. My brother Stan's delicate white baby dress was never the same.

As a grownup, Betty has never had a cat of her own that I can remember—but she has had dogs that she loves. She has a little stroller for her current dog, Lucy. She doesn't dress Lucy up or try to wipe her nose (that I know of) but Lucy likes the stroller a lot better than Tiger liked the buggy.

All these years later, I can still see that cat streaking up the tree.

Biographies

Celena Diana Bumpus, BA, AODA is the founder of three publishing houses. She teaches three creative writing classes at the Janet Goeske Senior Center in Riverside, Ca. She is the published author of the poetry collection, *Confessions* (1998, The Inevitable Press). Her personal essay was published in *Street Lit: Representing the Urban Landscape* (2014, Scarecrow Press). Her poetry has appeared in the following publications: *2012 Writing From Inlandia* (2012, Heyday Books), *Verse/Chorus: A Call and Response Anthology* (2013, Scarecrow Press), *2013 Writing From Inlandia* (2013, Heyday Books), *Invisible Memoirs* (2014, Memoir Journal), *Orangelandia: The Literature of Inlandia Citrus* (2014, Inlandia Institute), *2014 Writing From Inlandia* (2014, Inlandia Institute), *Pen 2 Paper Online Journal* (2014), *On The Rusk magazine* (2015), and *2015 Writing From Inlandia* (2015, Inlandia Institute). She is a member of six Inland Empire writing groups and has featured in several literary venues throughout Southern California. She is an avid blogger and a social media specialist. She was the host of the popular "Dreams Within The Ocean Literary Venue" in Corona, Ca and "Drownin' Mermaids Open Mic" in Riverside, Ca. Her website is www.islandsforwriters.blogspot.com. Visit her profile for her social media links.

Deenaz P. Coachbuilder, Ph.D is an educator, artist, poet and environmental advocate. She is a retired school principal and professor in special education, and a consulting speech pathologist. Deenaz is a Fulbright scholar, and the recipient of numerous awards, most recently, President Barak Obama's

"Volunteer Service" award. Deenaz's poetry, commentaries and essays have appeared in national and regional publications and poetry blogs in the U.S. and India. Her recent book of poems, *Imperfect Fragments*, has been received with critical acclaim both here and abroad. Deenaz has exhibited her paintings in oil in diverse venues, including a solo show. Deenaz resides in Riverside, Seattle and Mumbai, India. She enjoys reading, traveling, gardening, going for long walks, family and close friends, staying involved in the Indian American community and the Zoroastrain Association of California. She particularly cherishes being a wife and mother, and a recent grandmother.

Laurel Cortés: At 17, I went to Mexico City alone to attend the University of Mexico. The experience changed my life and, after majoring in Spanish and minoring in Comparative Literature at San Diego State University, I worked for 28 years at the University of California, Riverside, in—guess what?—the Department of Literatures and Languages. the job perfectly suited my interests, and it's fun now to do a bit of writing on my own.

Carlos Cortés is a professor emeritus of history at the University of California, Riverside. His most recent books are his memoir, *Rose Hill: An Intermarriage before Its Time* (Berkeley, CA: Heyday, 2012) and *Fourth Quarter: Reflections of a Cranky Old Man* (Los Angeles: Bad Knee Press, 2016). Other books include *The Children Are Watching: How the Media Teach about Diversity and The Making—and Remaking—of a Multiculturalist*, published by Teachers College Press. Cortes is general editor of *Multicultural America: A Multimedia Encyclopedia* (Sage, 2013), and Creative/Cultural Advisor for Nickelodeon's Peabody-award-winning children's television series, "Dora the Explorer," and its sequel, "Go,

Diego, Go!," for which he received the 2009 NAACP Image Award. He also travels the country performing his one-person autobiographical play, A Conversation with Alana: One Boy's Multicultural Rite of Passage, while he co-wrote the book and lyrics for the musical, *We Are Not Alone: Tomas Rivera—A Musical Narrative*, which premiered in 2011.

Ellen Estilai received her B.A. in Art from the University of California, Davis, and her M. A. in English Language and Literature from the University of Tehran. A former executive director of the Riverside Arts Council and the Arts Council for San Bernardino County, she has taught literature and writing at the University of Tehran, Cal State Bakersfield and the University of San Francisco's external degree program. Her essay, "Front Yard Fruit," originally published in *Alimentum: The Literature of Food*, is included in *New California Writing 2011* (Heyday) and was selected as a Notable Essay in *The Best American Essays 2011*. Her poetry and essays have also appeared in the journals *Phantom Seed, Broad!, Snapdragon: A Journal of Art and Healing,* and *Heron Tree,* and in the anthologies *Slouching Towards Mount Rubidoux Manor, (In)Visible Memoirs Vol. 2, Writing from Inlandia,* and *HOME: Tall Grass Writers Guild Anthology.*

Nan Friedley is a retired special education teacher originally from Indiana. She has participated in the Riverside Inlandia workshop for the past two years along with other local writing groups. Her poetry has been published in the 2013 Inlandia anthology and "Three" by PushPen Press. Thanks to fellow workshop members and leaders for the encouragement you've given me to keep writing.

liz gonzález grew up in the San Bernardino area. She writes poetry, fiction, and memoir, and her work has been published widely. Her poems are forthcoming or have recently appeared in *Askew Poetry Journal,* and *Cultural Weekly,* and in the anthologies *The Coiled Serpent* and *Wide Awake.* Excerpts from her novel-in-progress are forthcoming or have recently appeared in *Litbreak Magazine* and *Inlandia: A Literary Journey.* liz's recent awards include a 2016 Incite / Insight Award from the Arts Council for Long Beach and an Irvine Fellowship at the Lucas Artists Residency Program. Currently, she lives in North Long Beach, California, with her Jack Chi buddy Chacho and sound artist Jorge Martin. She directs Uptown Word & Arts and is a member of the Macondo Workshop. She works as a writing consultant and teaches creative writing through Angels Gate Cultural Center and UCLA Extension Writers' Program. www.lizgonzalez.com

Kamelyta Noor: I've always enjoyed writing, and telling stories. Apparently I have a fascinating life, so people always urge me to write about it. There's also the interesting fact that I've had at least 6 fortune tellers predicting that I'd be a famous writer in my 40s! Which is now! So here I am!

Jane O'Shields-Hayner is a writer and visual artist. She writes essays, non-fiction, biographical and historical fiction, and poetry; and she produces and shows visual art. In both art forms she addresses universal issues and their relationship to all of life and individual life journeys. Jane has bachelor's degrees in Fine Arts, with a specialty in art, and in education, from Texas Christian University. She also has a Master's degree in Occupational Therapy from Loma Linda University. Jane has a background in teaching art and other subjects in community and global activism. She practices occupational therapy with a specialty in home health care throughout Riverside County. Jane's husband, Bill Hayner is also an artist, an activist and an educator. They have two young children and two adult daughters and they live in Corona, in the foothills of the Santa Ana Mountains. She and her family are members of the Inland Valley Monthly Meeting of the Religious Society of Friends, also known as Quakers. Jane's work has recently been published in *Tiferet Journal*, *Friends Journal*, and *The Manifest Station*. She has recently shown artwork in The Studio Door Gallery in San Diego and other venues.

Christine Pence is an adult third culture kid whose professional work in aircraft spares support gave her the opportunity to travel widely after her university studies in business. Recently joining the Inlandia Writing Workshops in her hometown, she is opening a new creative outlet for sharing her adventures of life after 60 through writing, photography and travel filming for television. Her exhibited photography is sold internationally. She lives in Riverside, California.

Suzanne Shimaya appreciates that the Inlandia workshop experience has given her the opportunity to revisit some long-neglected fiction projects. She would especially like to thank Inlandia workshop leader and fiction writer Charlotte Davidson and poet Cathy Henley-Erickson for their gentle advice on story revision and for their encouragement.

As a clinical psychologist and spiritual director, **Judith E. Turian, Ph.D.** assists her clients by helping them establish or deepen their spiritual lives. While on active duty in the US Navy, Dr. Turian was the clinical director of the Alcoholic Rehabilitation Service at the Naval Hospital in Long Beach, CA where she was influenced by the power of Twelve Step spirituality. Based on her personal life and clinical experience, her book *God: A Relationship Guide*, helps people establish and deepen a relationship with God. Judith pursues her own spiritual growth through retreats. The silent retreat described in "Silence Spoken Here" took place at the New Camaldoni Hermitage, Big Sur, CA.

Gudelia Vaden (Delia) is a retired preschool teacher with a BA degree in Liberal Studies with a Bilingual-Bicultural Emphasis. In retirement, she has developed several hobbies: gardening, line dancing, watercolor painting and creative writing. During the last several years, she has participated in the Inlandia Creative Writing Workshops. Delia resides in Riverside, CA with her husband Tom and granddaughter Natasha. She has a son in Riverside and her daughter lives in San Francisco. Delia and Tom enjoy walking their Chihuahua (Pepper) in their Hillcrest neighborhood.

Tom Vaden is a retired statistician with a MS degree in Mathematics from the University of Missouri. In retirement, he has taken up several new hobbies: gardening, line dancing, and creative writing. During the last several years, he has participated in the Inlandia Creative Writing Workshops where he has learned much from the lively discussions and suggestions of the other participants. He resides in Riverside, CA with his wife Delia and a black and white very spoiled Chihuahua named Pepper. Tom has a daughter Natalie living in San Francisco, and a son Patrick living in Riverside – both are excellent writers. His granddaughter, Natasha, a graduate of the University of Oregon, lives with Delia and Tom.

Frances J. Vasquez resides in Riverside. She has a diverse background in public service, and was the Executive Director of Other Cultures, Inc., an international student exchange program specializing in exchanges between Mexico, Central America, Canada, and the U.S. She attended Inland schools and graduated with BS and MBA degrees from the University of California, Riverside. An aficionada of arts and letters, Frances enjoys attending and organizing cultural events.

Mae Wagner has lived in the Inlandia area since 1957 and has been a member of the Inlandia workshop since it's beginning in 2008. She is a mother of three, grandmother of seven and great-grandmother of four. She writes under her maiden name after having been married a couple of times too many. She lives in Redlands with her husband, Alex Marinello and her dog Sophie.

About the Inlandia Institute

The Inlandia Institute is a regional non-profit literary center. We seek to bring focus to the richness of the literary enterprise that has existed in this region for ages. The mission of the Inlandia Institute is to recognize, support and expand literary activity in all of its forms through community programs in the Inland Southern California, thereby deepening people's awareness, understanding, and appreciation of this unique, complex and creatively vibrant region.

The Institute publishes high quality regional writing in print and electronic form including books published in partnership with Heyday under the Inlandia Institute imprint as well as independent Inlandia Institute publications. The Inlandia Institute is also home to the Hillary Gravendyk prize, a national and regional poetry book competition.

Inlandia presents free public literary programming featuring authors who live in, work in, and/or write about Inland Southern California.

We also provide Creative Literacy Programs for children and youth and hold creative writing workshops for teens and adults.

In addition, every two years the Inlandia Institute appoints a distinguished jury panel from outside of the region to name an Inlandia Literary Laureate who serves as an ambassador for the Inlandia Institute, promoting literature, creative literacy, and community throughout the entire Inlandia region. To date, Laureates include Susan Straight (2010-12), Gayle Brandeis (2012-14), Juan Delgado (2014-16), and Nikia Chaney (2016-2018).

To learn more about the Inlandia Institute please visit our website at www.InlandiaInstitute.org.

Other Inlandia Publications

Inlandia Books - Literary
All Things Lose Thousands of Times
Angela Peñaredondo
Winner of the Regional Hillary Gravendyk Prize

Map of an Onion
Kenji C. Liu
Winner of the National Hillary Gravendyk Prize

Inlandia Books - Community
No Easy Way: Integrating Riverside Schools – A Victory for Community
Arthur L. Littleworth
Edited by Dawn Hassett
Foreword by Dr. V.P. Franklin
Introduction by Susan Straight

Tia's Tamale Trouble
Julianna Cruz, author
Tracie Lents, illustrator

Orangelandia: The Literature of Inland Citrus
Edited by Gayle Brandeis

Dos Chiles/Two Chilies
Julianna Cruz

Yearly, 2011-2015 Writing from Inlandia:
Work of the Inlandia Creative Writing Writing Workshops
Edited by the Inlandia Institute Publications Committee

Heyday Inlandia Imprint Books

Empire
Lewis deSoto

Vital Signs
Juan Delgado and Thomas McGovern

Rose Hill: An Intermarriage before Its Time
Carlos Cortès

No Place for a Puritan: The Literature of California's Deserts
Edited by Ruth Nolan

Backyard Birds of the Inland Empire
Sheila N. Kee

Dream Street
Douglas F. McCulloh

Inlandia: A Literary Journey Through California's Inland Empire
Edited by Gayle Wattawa with an introduction by Susan Straight

Inlandia Electronic Publications

Inlandia: A Literary Journey, an on-line journal
Edited by Lawrence Eby